Dubrovsky

and

Egyptian Nights

Alexander Pushkin

Translated by Robert Chandler

ET REMOTISSIMA PROPE

100 PAGES

100 PAGES
Published by Hesperus Press Limited
4 Rickett Street, London SW6 1RU
www.hesperuspress.com

Dubrovsky first published in Russian in 1841; 'Egyptian Nights'
first published in Russian in 1837
This translation first published by Hesperus Press Limited, 2003

Introduction and English language translation © Robert Chandler, 2003
Foreword © Patrick Neate, 2003

Designed and typeset by Fraser Muggeridge
Printed in the United Arab Emirates by Oriental Press

ISBN: 1-84391-053-5

CONTENTS

Approaching *Dubrovsky*, it is, I think, hard not to ponder the gulf between yourself and the text. I know this is a comment you can make of any reading (from great literature to shopping catalogues) but in this case it does seem particularly pertinent.

For starters – even dismissing obvious distances of time and geography – you are reading in translation. And this is not just any translation either, but that of a celebrated poet's rare prose. So aren't you inevitably destined to miss a nuance or two? What's more, Pushkin was not so much part of a literary movement as its progenitor. He was the first to write in Russian vernacular, he revelled in flouting convention, he was at the heartbeat of a nascent revolutionary politics and he paved the way for the likes of Gogol, Turgenev and Lermontov. What are you to make of all that? Finally, of course, this novella was unfinished, so, at the outset, you're already wondering how it otherwise might have looked.

With all the above in mind, therefore, I came to this story with some degree of trepidation. Without trawling paperweights of social history and reams of secondary literature, how could I possibly get to grips with it? I needn't have worried.

It goes without saying that one mark of great writing is its capacity to transcend its socio-historical context. It is notable, too, that the themes and characters of nineteenth-century Russian literature – whether you're talking about the moral apathy of Lermontov's Pechorin or Dostoevsky's great anti-hero, Raskolnikov – often seem almost preternaturally modern. Nonetheless, after several re-readings, I remain astonished by the resonance and relevance of Pushkin's *Dubrovsky*.

Once (and only once) I attended a day's creative-writing course. Among the numerous sound bites spouted by the tutor, one was brought to mind by this story: 'Show, don't tell.' Despite my basic distrust of aphorisms, I *do* know what the tutor was getting at – allow the characters the space to reveal themselves by word and deed. But it is striking that, in *Dubrovsky*, Pushkin never fails to tell us exactly what's going on.

In the very first paragraph, we meet Troekurov. He's the evil landowner, the 'baddie'. Pushkin may not quite use that word but he does immediately depict him as a satyr and a man who gives 'free rein to every impulse of his hot-blooded nature and every whim of his somewhat limited mind'. Later, when we come to 'the real hero', the younger Dubrovsky, that is *precisely* how Pushkin introduces him; while Masha too, Troekurov's daughter, is welcomed as 'the heroine of our tale'. It took me some time to admit that there is nothing clumsy about these descriptions. Rather it is as if Pushkin wants to get the archetypes out of the way in order to get on to more interesting stuff.

Dubrovsky, you see, has much of the structure of mythology; a strong moral purpose that is played out through its characters. Troekurov tricks his former friend (Dubrovsky senior) out of his property; an injustice that destroys him. The friend's son returns from the military and plans vengeance through a fiendish plot. But this dashing young fellow's heart is turned when he falls in love with Troekurov's daughter; a model of beauty and virtue. It's fairy-tale stuff and that goes part of the way to explain its enduring charm.

And yet Pushkin also locates his fairy tale in reality with dry precision. His economy of language is breathtaking as the reader is pitched into the midst of Russian rural life and its class system, both subtle and grotesque. Rarely can cynicism – typically the coldest of devices – have lent such life to a story. When Masha meets her new tutor, for example, we are told that 'a servant or artisan, in her eyes, was not a man'. Similarly the Prince, her suitor, is described as 'perpetually bored' and in 'perpetual need for distraction'. Only the younger Dubrovsky is granted an ounce of tenderness as he reads through his dead mother's letters to his dead father; a relationship already curtailed.

But Pushkin's intention is not just to cut the Russian establishment down to size with a razor-sharp turn of phrase or two. No.

Great fairy tales are typically about integration. They posit a situation of fantastical social disharmony and then resolve it through the story. Pushkin, however, uses the medium's narrative form with serious and specific political intent: to reveal the inequity of the law.

Dubrovsky senior loses his estate to Troekurov not through any fault of his own but through a court judgement that plays to the whims of the local bigwig. The law, we are shown, is friend only to the powerful.

Indeed, Pushkin's adaptation of a real legal document demonstrates his delight in bumping his reader from fairy tale to hard fact: 'We quote it [the judgement] in full, believing everyone will be pleased to learn of one of the methods by which a man in Russia can be deprived of an estate to which he has indisputable rights.' It is this judgement that forces the young Dubrovsky now to live outside the law, as a 'brigand'. Of course he then falls in love with the beautiful Masha. But does that guarantee his fairy-tale reintegration? I doubt Pushkin ever considered such a cuddly outcome.

A couple of observations.

Bankrupted by the law, the young Dubrovsky is propelled into a half-world between nobility and serfdom, and Pushkin surely felt great affinity with his protagonist. Pushkin himself was born into the second tier of Russian society. Though raised and educated (like all his class) in French, he learnt Russian from the labourers on his father's estate and, through his nanny, became fascinated by traditional folk tales. Later, after years of exile for his political poetry, he returned to a humble position in the Moscow Court of Tsar Nicholas I and married a noted society beauty. It was an unhappy marriage, and he was eventually killed in a duel defending her honour.

It seems to me, therefore, that both *Dubrovsky* the story and its eponymous hero are reflective of the author. Pushkin writes sensitively of the common man and scathingly of the establishment. How eloquently this speaks of his own uncertain social position. As for Dubrovsky, I cannot help but think that Pushkin would have loved to be a handsome outlaw (as opposed to a short genius who once described himself as having 'a proper monkey's face'!). How readily Pushkin would have swapped his own tragedy for that of his character; tragedies that both resonate still.

And doesn't the politics seem similarly contemporary and compelling? Picturing Pushkin's rural Russia, I found myself imagining something like a federation of village states, each under the rule of a patriarch, more or less evil, more or less powerful, more or less concerned for the well-being of his disenfranchised citizens. These patriarchs are, of course, theoretically beholden to what, in my model, you might call 'international law'. But the reality is that this law only really serves those with the most power and patronage. And whatever the outcome of the patriarchs' squabbles, it's the common men who can expect to suffer most. It is, I suggest, hard to ignore the continuing currency of Pushkin's underlying hypothesis. *Dubrovsky* shows that the work of Russia's greatest poet is as resonant and relevant as ever.

– Patrick Neate, 2003

Pushkin's importance in Russian literature is even greater than that of Shakespeare and Dante in their respective national literatures. He perhaps has more in common with Goethe. Not only is he Russia's greatest poet; he is also the author of the first major works in a variety of genres. As well as his masterpieces – the verse novel *Eugene Onegin* and the narrative poem *The Bronze Horseman* – Pushkin wrote one of the first important Russian dramas, *Boris Godunov*, the finest Russian historical novel, *The Captain's Daughter*, and the greatest of all Russian short stories, *The Queen of Spades*.

Pushkin's first popular success was the Romantic narrative poem *Ruslan and Ludmila*, published in 1820. He began writing prose only in 1827, and he worked on *Dubrovsky* between October 1832 and February 1833. His prose style is clear, clean and succinct; he himself wrote that: 'Precision and brevity are the most important qualities of prose. Prose demands thoughts and more thoughts – without thoughts, dazzling expressions serve no purpose.' *Dubrovsky*, however, is so very simply and concisely written that it is easy for the reader to lose sight of its fundamental seriousness. Like *The Captain's Daughter*, it is an account of a seemingly inevitable conflict and a plea for the importance of reconciliation.

As in all his work, Pushkin seldom moralises or makes overt judgements. The irony with which he introduces the long legal document (a transcript of a judgement made by a Russian court in 1832 – Pushkin has changed only names and dates) is therefore all the more striking. Given that the judicial tradition is entirely corrupt, the only hope for a solution to the conflict between Troekurov and the Dubrovskys lies either in their own consciences or in the benign workings of patriarchal tradition. The cruel and arrogant General Troekurov attempts, rather late in the day, to act according to his conscience, but its voice is silenced by a combination of his own pride and chance events. As for patriarchal tradition, the old nurse's trust in the Tsar is comically misplaced: the Tsar, needless to say, has no interest in the small village of Kistenevka. Other fatherly figures are more actively malign: Troekurov uses his authority to tyrannise family, neighbours, serfs, serf-girls and even bears. The only benign patriarch, ironically, is the young Dubrovsky – in his relationship with his fellow-brigands and even with some of his potential victims.

The conflict between the two families appears to have a fated quality. Words such as 'war', 'enemy' and 'brigand' are bandied about from the very beginning of the quarrel; even the name of the Dubrovskys' estate, Kistenevka, is related to a phrase meaning 'to plunder'. The conflict can, however, be explained psychologically. The two inseparable friends, Troekurov and the elder Dubrovsky, are simply too similar: both are proud, independent, and unable to compromise or forgive. As for Vladimir Dubrovsky, he has much in common with his elders; it is his pride and courage that turn him into a rebel. At the same time, these qualities endear him, in his disguise as French tutor, not only to Troekurov but also to his daughter Masha. In the end, Vladimir is enabled by his love of Masha to forgive Troekurov and so break a terrible cycle of pride, vengefulness and enmity.

Dubrovsky has a satisfying shape as it stands, but it is nevertheless unfinished. We do not know why Pushkin abandoned work on the novel, and we have only the briefest of indications as to how he intended it to continue. One note runs: 'Life of Maria Kirilovna. Death of Prince Vereisky. The widow. The Englishman. Meeting. Gamblers. The chief of police. Conclusion.' The other runs: 'Moscow, a healer, solitude. Tavern, denunciation. Suspicions, the chief of police.' It seems likely that 'the Englishman' is Dubrovsky in yet another disguise, but the nature of the conclusion itself remains a mystery.

Egyptian Nights is among the finest, if most fragmentary, of Pushkin's works. Like *Dubrovsky*, it was published only after his death. The prose sections were probably written in autumn 1835; the first passage of verse incorporates lines from a poem written in 1832, *Yezersky*; the second passage of verse is an expansion of a poem about Cleopatra written in 1828. Like the poet evoked by his mysterious Italian *improvvisatore*, Pushkin handles quick changes of tone and subject matter with elegance and grace. The witty description of the audience's behaviour before the *improvvisatore*'s performance gives us a vivid glimpse of high-society St Petersburg. Pushkin's portrayal of Charsky, and of his awkward relationship to his calling, is fascinating –

all the more so since Pushkin has clearly endowed Charsky with at least some traits of his own character. There is subtle discussion, in both verse and prose, of the poet's place in society and his responsibilities to his art. Another important theme is the interdependency of poise and awkwardness. Both Charsky and the *improvvisatore* slip between extremes of poised fluency and deep embarrassment; and the plain, awkward girl who (probably) proposes the theme of '*Cleopatra e i suoi amanti*' is contrasted with the Cleopatra-like beauty who finally reads aloud what the girl has (probably) written. The work ends with a passage of narrative verse that is impassioned yet deftly controlled. The idea that men might be ready to accept execution in exchange for a night with Cleopatra appears at first to be the height of Romanticism; with a slight shock, however, we discover that Flavius, at least, is moved not by passion for Cleopatra but by fury at her arrogance. *Egyptian Nights*, in short, is dense with delicate contrasts, parallels and paradoxes. The topic assigned to the Italian for his first improvisation is that no poet should be assigned topics; the Italian then demonstrates, through his fluency, the opposite of what his words assert. The audience that gathers to hear his second improvisation is at first unresponsive – just as the audience he describes in this improvisation is at first unresponsive to Cleopatra. Cleopatra's lovers, like the *improvvisatore*, are called upon to surrender themselves. Cleopatra herself, however, also proves to have something in common with the *improvvisatore*; like him, she is a gifted artist, able to divine a man's hidden wishes. There is even a hint, in the very last line, that love may force even her to surrender herself. Almost everything in *Egyptian Nights* is surprising. The work's only flaw is that it ends so soon; like Shakespeare's Cleopatra, Pushkin 'makes hungry where most [he] satisfies'.

I am grateful to the following, all of whom have painstakingly read through drafts and made useful suggestions: my wife, Elizabeth Chandler; Leon Burnett; Olive Classe; Musya Dmitrovskaya; Olga Meerson; Mark Miller. Many of my thoughts about *Egyptian Nights* are inspired by remarks made by my niece, Lucy Chandler, just as many of my thoughts about *Dubrovsky* are borrowed from a fine article by N. Zhilina, published in the *Baltiiskii filologicheskii kuryer* (Kaliningrad, 2000, vol. 1). I am also grateful to Norma Rinsler and Daniel Weissbort for publishing extracts from *Egyptian Nights* in issue 21 of their excellent journal *Modern Poetry in Translation*.

– *Robert Chandler, 2003*

Dubrovsky

Volume One

1

Several years ago, on one of his estates, there lived a Russian gentleman of the old school, Kirila Petrovich Troekurov. His wealth, connections and distinguished lineage made him an important figure in the provinces where his estates were situated. His neighbours were glad to indulge his slightest whims and local officials trembled when they heard his name. Kirila Petrovich accepted these signs of servility as his due; his house was always full of guests willing to share in his noisy, sometimes even riotous pursuits and so help him while away his hours of gentlemanly leisure. No one dared turn down an invitation from him or ventured not to come to Pokrovskoye, on certain days of the year, to pay his respects. In his domestic life Kirila Petrovich exhibited all the vices of a man without education. Spoiled by everything around him, he was accustomed to giving free rein to every impulse of his hot-blooded nature and every whim of his somewhat limited mind. Despite his unusually strong constitution, he suffered from the effects of gluttony about twice every week, and he was tipsy every evening. In one wing of his house he kept sixteen chambermaids – sewing, embroidering and working at other ladylike tasks. The windows in this wing were protected by wooden bars; the doors were secured by locks whose keys were in the keeping of Kirila Petrovich. At appointed hours the young recluses, watched over by two old women, went out for walks in the garden. Now and again Kirila Petrovich would give some of them away in marriage, and new ones would take their place. His treatment of his peasants and house serfs was severe and wilful; yet they were proud of their master's wealth and reputation, and they in turn took many liberties with their neighbours, trusting in his powerful protection.

Troekurov invariably spent his days riding on horseback about his extensive estates, enjoying prolonged feasts and playing pranks, new examples of which he invented daily and whose victim was usually some new acquaintance, although even old friends were not always spared – with the single exception of Andrey Gavrilovich Dubrovsky. This Dubrovsky, a retired Guards lieutenant, was his closest neighbour, and the owner of seventy serfs. Troekurov, arrogant in his dealings with people of the very highest rank, was always respectful towards Dubrovsky in spite of the latter's humble standing. At one time they had served together, and Troekurov remembered his former comrade's intolerance and resoluteness only too well. Circumstances, however, had separated them for many years. Dubrovsky, his estate in disorder, had had no choice but to retire from the Guards and settle down in what remained of his village. Kirila Petrovich, learning of this, had offered him assistance, but Dubrovsky had thanked him and remained poor and independent. Some years later, Troekurov, by then a captain general, also retired to his estate; they met again and were overjoyed to see one another. Since then, they had met together every day, and Kirila Petrovich, who had never in his life graced anyone with a visit, would call at his friend's little house without the least ceremony. They were of the same age, they had been born into the same social class, they had received the same education, and they also had much in common with regard to character and general disposition. In some respects their fates had been similar: both had married for love, both had soon been widowed and each had been left with a single child. Dubrovsky's son was being educated in St Petersburg, while Troekurov's daughter was being brought up at home; Troekurov often used to say to Dubrovsky, 'Listen, brother Andrey Gavrilovich, if your Volodka grows up with a head on his shoulders, he can marry my Masha. Never mind if he's as poor as a church mouse.' Andrey Gavrilovich would shake his head and answer, 'No, Kirila Petrovich. My Volodka's no husband for your Maria Kirilovna. A poor gentleman like him is better off marrying a poor gentlewoman – and being head of the household – than marrying a spoilt hussy and ending up as her steward.'

Everyone envied the harmony between the arrogant Troekurov and his poor neighbour, and everyone marvelled at the latter's boldness when he spoke out straightforwardly at Kirila Petrovich's table, not worrying whether his opinions contradicted his host's. Some tried to imitate him, stepping beyond the boundaries of due subservience, but Kirila Petrovich gave them such a fright that no one ever dared do anything of the kind again, and Dubrovsky alone remained outside the law. Everything, however, was turned upside down by an unexpected event.

Early one autumn, Kirila Petrovich was making preparations to go hunting. The day before the hunt, the grooms and kennel-men were ordered to be ready by five o'clock the following morning. A tent and a field kitchen were sent ahead to the place where Kirila Petrovich expected to dine. Meanwhile, the host and his guests went out to look at the kennels, where over five hundred hounds and borzois lived in comfort and warmth, praising Kirila Petrovich's generosity in their canine tongue. There was not only a hospital for sick dogs, under the supervision of staff physician Timoshka, but also a section where noble bitches whelped and suckled their puppies. Kirila Petrovich was proud of this splendid establishment and never missed a chance to show it off to his guests, each of whom had already inspected it at least twenty times. Surrounded by his guests and accompanied by Timoshka and the chief kennel-men, Kirila Petrovich strolled slowly round; stopping outside particular kennels, he would ask questions about the health of sick dogs, make observations of varying degrees of justice and severity, or call out to dogs he knew and talk to them affectionately. The guests considered it their duty to express their admiration. Only Dubrovsky frowned and said nothing. He was a passionate hunter. His circumstances allowed him to keep only two hounds and one pack of borzois; he couldn't but feel a certain envy at the sight of this magnificent establishment. 'Why are you frowning, brother?' Kirila Petrovich asked him. 'Do you not like my kennels?' 'No,' Dubrovsky answered sullenly, 'your kennels are wonderful. I doubt if your servants live as well as your dogs.' One of the kennel-men took exception to this. 'Thanks be to God and to our master,' he said, 'we have no complaints, but in all truth there are gentlemen who'd be onto a good thing if they could exchange their estates for any one of these here kennels. They'd be warmer – and better fed.' Kirila Petrovich laughed loudly at his serf's impudent remark, and his guests laughed too, even though they each felt that the man's joke might have been directed at him in person. Dubrovsky went pale and said nothing. Just then some newborn puppies were brought to Kirila Petrovich in a basket, and for a while they took up his attention; he chose two to keep and ordered the rest to be drowned. In the meantime Dubrovsky disappeared, and no one noticed.

On returning from the kennels, Kirila Petrovich and his guests sat down to supper; only then did Kirila Petrovich realise his friend was missing. He gave orders: Dubrovsky was to be brought back without fail; someone must catch up with him immediately. Never in his life had he been hunting without Dubrovsky, an experienced and discriminating judge of canine merits and an unerring adjudicator of every possible kind of hunting dispute. The servant sent galloping after Dubrovsky appeared while they were still at table; he reported to his master that Andrey Gavrilovich had refused to listen and had not returned with him. Kirila Petrovich, excited as he usually was after drinking liqueurs, was enraged. He sent the same servant back after Andrey Gavrilovich to tell him he must return to Pokrovskoye at once and stay the night; should Andrey Gavrilovich fail to do this, then he, Troekurov, would sever relations with him for ever. The servant galloped off again. Kirila Petrovich got up from the table and, leaving his guests to find their way to their rooms, retired to bed.

His first question the following morning was: 'Is Andrey Gavrilovich here?' By way of an answer he was given a letter, folded into a triangle. Kirila Petrovich ordered his scribe to read it and heard the following:

'*Most gracious sir,*
I do not intend to visit Pokrovskoye until you send me your huntsman Paramoshka with an admission of his guilt; whether I punish or pardon him will be at my pleasure and I do not intend to endure jests from your serfs and I will not endure them from you, since I myself am no clown but a nobleman of ancient lineage. Meanwhile I remain your humble servant,

Andrey Dubrovsky'

By today's standards of etiquette, this letter would be considered most vulgar; Kirila Petrovich, however, was angered not by its strange style and composition but by its substance. 'What!' he thundered, leaping out of bed in his bare feet, 'I'm to send him my men with admissions of guilt and it will be his pleasure to punish or pardon them! What's got into the man? Who does he take me for? I'll show him. He'll live to regret this – I'll teach him how to treat a Troekurov!'

Kirila Petrovich dressed and rode out in his usual splendour, but the hunt was unsuccessful. They saw only one hare during the entire day, and it escaped. Dinner in the open fields under a tent was also unsuccessful, or at least not to the taste of Kirila Petrovich, who thrashed his cook and tongue-lashed his guests; on the way home, together with the whole hunt, he deliberately rode over Dubrovsky's fields.

Several days passed, and the enmity between the two neighbours did not abate. Dubrovsky did not go to Pokrovskoye. Kirila Petrovich was bored and lonely without him, and his irritation poured out in the most abusive expressions which, thanks to the zeal of the local landowners, reached Dubrovsky with amendments and embellishments of all kinds. Any last hope of reconciliation was destroyed by another incident.

Dubrovsky was riding round his small estate; nearing a birch copse, he heard the blows of an axe and, a minute later, the crash of a falling tree. He hurried into the copse and found peasants from Pokrovskoye, calmly stealing his timber. Seeing him, they tried to run off. Dubrovsky and his coachman caught two of them, bound them and brought them back to the house. The victor's spoils also included three enemy horses. Dubrovsky was extremely angry: Troekurov's men, known brigands, were aware of his friendship with their master and had never before dared get up to mischief on his property. Dubrovsky realised they were taking advantage of the recent breach in relations, and he decided, contrary to all the conventions of war, to teach his prisoners a lesson, using the switches they had cut in his copse, and to appropriate the three horses, putting them to work alongside his own.

Word of this event reached Kirila Petrovich that same day. He was beside himself and, in his first moments of fury, wanted to muster his house serfs, attack Kistenevka (as his neighbour's village was called), raze it to the ground and besiege the landlord himself in his house. To him such a feat would have been nothing unusual. But his thoughts were soon taken in a different direction.

Pacing heavy-footed up and down the hall, he happened to glance out of the window and see a troika that had stopped by the gate; a small man in a leather cap and an overcoat of coarse frieze got out of the cart and went into a wing of the house to see the steward. Troekurov recognised Shabashkin, the assessor, and sent for him. Within a minute

Shabashkin was standing before Kirila Petrovich, bowing low bows and reverently awaiting his orders.

'Good day, Mister Whatever-your-name-is!' said Troekurov. 'What's brought you to us?'

'I was on my way to town, Your Excellency,' said Shabashkin, 'and I called in on Ivan Demyanov to see if Your Excellency had any orders.'

'You've come just at the right time, Mister Whatever-your-name-is; I need you. Have some vodka and listen!'

The assessor was pleasantly amazed by the warmth of this welcome. He refused the vodka and listened to Kirila Petrovich with all his attention.

'I have a neighbour,' said Troekurov, 'a boor of a small landowner. I want to take his estate from him. What do you think?'

'Your Excellency, if you have some documents or…'

'Nonsense, my brother, what do we want with documents? What are court decrees for? How, I need to know, without having any right to it, can I confiscate his estate? But wait a moment… The estate did once belong to us. We bought it from some fellow called Spitsyn, then sold it to Dubrovsky's father. Can't we make something of that?'

'It would be difficult, Your Highest Excellency. The sale was probably effected in a legal manner.'

'Think, brother. Rack your brains.'

'If, for example, Your Excellency could somehow obtain from your neighbour the record or deed entitling him to his estate, then of course…'

'I understand – but the documents, unfortunately, were burnt during a fire.'

'What, Your Excellency! The documents were burnt? What more could you ask for? In that case, you may proceed in accordance with the law, and there is no doubt you will receive your complete satisfaction.'

'You think so? Well then, take good care. I rely on your zeal, and you may be assured of my gratitude.'

Shabashkin bowed almost to the ground, drove away, and set to work that very day; it was thanks to his expeditiousness that, just two weeks later, Dubrovsky was requested by the authorities to provide them at once with an adequate explanation of how he had come to be in possession of the village of Kistenevka.

Amazed by this unexpected request, Andrey Gavrilovich immediately wrote a rather rude reply, stating that the village of Kistenevka had come to him on the death of his father, that he held it by right of inheritance, that none of this was any of Troekurov's business, and that any other party's claims to the property were a slander and fraud.

The impression made by this letter on Shabashkin, the assessor, was an extremely agreeable one. He could see, firstly, that Dubrovsky knew little about legal matters, and, secondly, that it would not be difficult to place someone so hot-tempered and incautious in an extremely awkward position. After considering the assessor's requests more coolly, Andrey Gavrilovich understood the need to reply in more detail. He wrote a fairly businesslike document, but even this was to prove inadequate.

The matter dragged on. Convinced of the rightness of his case, Andrey Gavrilovich troubled himself very little about it; he had neither the wish nor the means to scatter money about, and, although he had always been the first to joke about how easy it was to buy the consciences of bureaucrats, it never occurred to him that he might himself become a victim of fraud. Troekurov, for his part, showed equally little concern about winning the case he had initiated. Shabashkin, however, busied himself on his behalf, acted in his name, intimidated and bribed judges, and interpreted every possible decree every which way.

In the event, on the ninth day of February 18**, Dubrovsky received from the town police a summons to appear before the *** District Judge in order to hear the latter's ruling on the matter of the estate disputed between him, Lieutenant Dubrovsky, and Captain General Troekurov, and to sign in testimony of his satisfaction or dissatisfaction. Dubrovsky left for town that same day; on the way he was overtaken by Troekurov. They exchanged haughty glances, and Dubrovsky saw a malicious smile on the face of his adversary.

2

On his arrival in town, Andrey Gavrilovich stopped at the house of a merchant he knew and stayed the night with him; the following morning he appeared at the District Court. No one paid any attention to him. Kirila Petrovich arrived just after him. The clerks rose to their feet and put their pens behind their ears. The members of the court met him with expressions of profound servility and pulled up an armchair for him out of respect for his rank, years and portliness. He sat down close to the door, which was left open. Still standing, Andrey Gavrilovich leant against the wall. A deep silence set in, and the secretary began to read out the court's judgement in a ringing voice. We quote it in full, believing everyone will be pleased to learn of one of the methods by which a man in Russia can be deprived of an estate to which he has indisputable rights:

On the 27th day of October in the year 18** the *** District Court examined the case of the wrongful possession by Guards Lieutenant Andrey, son of Gavril, Dubrovsky, of an estate belonging to Captain General Kirila, son of Pyotr, Troekurov, and which comprises the village of Kistenevka in the *** province, male serfs to the number of ***, and *** acres of land with meadows and all appurtenances. Concerning which matter it is evident that: on the 9th day of June in the past year of 18**, the said Captain General Troekurov lodged a petition with this court, stating that, on the 14th day of August 17**, his late father, a Knight and Collegiate Assessor, Pyotr, son of Yefim, Troekurov, then serving with the rank of Provincial Secretary in the *** Vicegerent's Chancery, did purchase from Chancery Clerk Fadey, son of Yegor, Spitsyn, of the nobility, the property comprising the aforesaid village of Kistenevka, (which village, at that time, according to the *** census, was known as the Kistenev settlement), and, according to the *** census, male serfs to the number of ***, together with all their peasants' chattels, and also arable and non-arable land, forests, hay meadows, the fishing in the river known as the Kistenevka, and all appurtenances of the above estate, together with a timber manorial house, and in short everything without remainder which

12

came to him by inheritance from his father Sergeant Yegor, son of Terenty, Spitsyn, of the nobility, and which he held in his possession, not excepting a single serf or a single acre of land, for a price of 2,500 roubles, for which a deed of sale was registered on that same day in the chambers of the *** Court and Tribunal, and his father, Collegiate Assessor, Pyotr, son of Yefim, Troekurov on that 26th day of August took possession of this estate, this being registered in the District Court. And lastly, on the 6th day of September in the year 17**, his father by the will of God passed away, while he himself, the aforesaid plaintiff Captain General Troekurov had, almost since his infancy, from the year 17**, been serving in the army, and for most of that time he had been campaigning in foreign lands, for which reason he was unable to receive intelligence either of his father's death or of the estate that had been left to him. Now, however, upon his final retirement from that service and his return to his father's estates, comprising, in the *** districts of the *** provinces, some several villages with 3,000 serfs in all, he discovers that one of these said villages with, according to the *** census, serfs to the number of *** (and according to the most recent census, serfs to the number of ***) is in the possession of the aforesaid Guards Lieutenant Andrey Dubrovsky, for which reason, presenting together with his petition the original deed of sale given to his father by the vendor, Spitsyn, he petitions that the aforesaid estate be removed from the wrongful possession of Dubrovsky and placed as it should be at his own full disposal. And with regard to the wrongful appropriation of the aforesaid estate, from which he has enjoyed revenues, he petitions that, after due investigation, lawful damages be exacted from Dubrovsky and satisfaction rendered to himself, Troekurov.

Investigations carried out by the *** District Court following upon this petition have revealed that: the aforesaid Guards Lieutenant Dubrovsky, currently in possession of the disputed estate, has deposed to the local Assessor of the Nobility that the estate currently in his possession, comprising the said village of Kistenevka, together with serfs to the number of *** and all land and appurtenances thereto, came into his possession by inheritance, upon the death of his father, Sub-Lieutenant in the Artillery Gavril, son of Yevgraf, Dubrovsky, who himself purchased the estate from the father of the plaintiff, *formerly Provincial Secretary and subsequently Collegiate Assessor Troekurov, this being effected through a procuration granted on the 30th day of August in the year 17** and notarised in the *** District Court to Titular Councillor Grigory, son of Vasily, Sobolev, according to which there must have been drawn up a deed of purchase of this estate by his father, since the said procuration states that he, Troekurov, had sold to Dubrovsky's father the entire estate, comprising serfs to the number of *** and land, and that he had received in full and not returned the 3,200 roubles due to him in accordance with their agreement, and that he had requested the aforementioned Sobolev to convey to him the said deed of purchase. This same procuration also stipulated that Dubrovsky's father, in consideration of his having paid the entire sum due, should take possession of the said estate and dispose of it as its rightful owner, even before the completion of the said deed of purchase, and that neither the vendor, Troekurov, nor any other person should henceforth interfere with the property. But when exactly and at which office the aforesaid deed of purchase was given to his father by the attorney Sobolev, he, Andrey Dubrovsky, did not know, having been at that time still a minor, and because after his father's death he was unable to find said deed of purchase and he supposes said deed to have been destroyed, along with other documents and property, in a fire that occurred in their house in the year 17**, and which the inhabitants of said village remember well. And that, since the day of the sale by Troekurov or of the issue of the procuration to Sobolev, that is since the year 17**, and following the death of his father in 17**, and up until the present day, the Dubrovskys have been in undisputed possession of this estate, to all of which the local inhabitants, 52 in number, have testified under oath that indeed, as they can well remember, the Dubrovskys first came into possession of the aforesaid estate seventy years previously, and without dispute, but by what deed or title they do not know. Whether the aforementioned prior purchaser of the estate, Pyotr Troekurov, formerly Provincial Secretary, enjoyed possession of this estate, they do not remember. The house in the possession of the Dubrovsky family did indeed burn down some thirty years ago, in a fire that took hold in the village at night; and it was generally reckoned that the annual revenue* *from the disputed estate, all in all, from that time until the present day, had amounted to no less than 2,000 roubles.*

In response, on the third day of January of the present year, Captain General Kirila, son of Pyotr, Troekurov petitioned this court to find that although the aforesaid Guards Lieutenant Andrey Dubrovsky had, in the course of this present investigation, submitted as evidence the procuration given by his late father Gavril Dubrovsky to Titular Councillor Sobolev with regard to the purchase of said estate, he had not, through this document, provided, as required by Chapter Nineteen of the General Regulations and by the edict of 29th November 1752, any genuine deed of title, or indeed any clear evidence of the execution, at any time, of such a deed. Wherefore, this same procuration, after the death of its issuer, his father, is, according to the edict of the *** day of May 1818, entirely invalid.

Moreover, it has been decreed that the ownership of disputed estates shall be determined according to deed of title, if such a deed exists, and according to the results of an investigation, if such a deed proves not to exist.

Captain General Kirila, son of Pyotr, Troekurov has already submitted in evidence a deed of title to the said estate, formerly belonging to his father, and he therefore petitions, on the basis of the laws aforementioned, that the estate be removed from the possession of the aforesaid Dubrovsky and restored to himself as the rightful owner thereof by right of inheritance. And since the aforesaid landowners, having in their possession an estate to which they had no right or title, have wrongfully enjoyed revenues from this estate to which they have no entitlement, it should be established by law to what sum these said revenues amount and this sum should be exacted from the landowner Dubrovsky and restored to him, Troekurov, to his entire satisfaction.

Concerning the said disputed estate, now in the possession of Guards Lieutenant Andrey, son of Gavril, Dubrovsky, and which comprises the village of Kistenevka and, according to the most recent census, male serfs to the number of ***, together with land and appurtenances, it is evident that Captain General Kirila, son of Pyotr, Troekurov, has submitted a valid deed of sale of the same, in the year 17**, by Chancery Clerk Fadey, son of Yegor, Spitsyn, of the nobility, to his own late father, formerly Provincial Secretary and afterwards Collegiate Assessor. Furthermore, the said purchaser of the estate, Troekurov, as appears from this title deed, was indeed that same year placed in possession of said estate by the *** District Court, with livery of seisin executed. And although Guards Lieutenant Dubrovsky has submitted in evidence a procuration given by the aforementioned deceased purchaser Troekurov to Titular Councillor Sobolev for the completion of a deed of purchase by his father Dubrovsky, it is nevertheless expressly forbidden by Statute *** not only to confirm ownership of immoveable real estate on such basis but even to enter into provisional ownership thereof; and moreover, the said procuration is itself rendered null and void by the death of its issuer. Furthermore, from the commencement of the present enquiry, that is, from the year 18**, and until the present day, no clear evidence has been submitted by Dubrovsky that any title deed in respect of the purchase of the said disputed estate was ever at any time or place completed. This Court therefore decrees: that the said estate, with serfs to the number of ***, with land and appurtenances, in whatsoever condition it should now be, be confirmed, in accordance with the title deed he has himself presented, as the property of Captain General Troekurov; that Guards Lieutenant Dubrovsky be removed from the possession of said estate; and that seisin be granted to Troekurov as by right of inheritance and that this be registered at the *** District Court. And, although Captain General Troekurov has furthermore petitioned for the exaction from Guards Lieutenant Dubrovsky of the revenues enjoyed by him as a result of his wrongful possession of said estate, nevertheless, since the said estate, according to the testimony of inhabitants of long standing, has been in the undisputed possession of the Dubrovsky family for some years, and since there is no evidence that Mr Troekurov has ever before, regarding the Dubrovskys' wrongful possession of the said estate, lodged any petition on the basis of the decree that should one man sow the land of another or fence round his property, and should a petition be made regarding this unlawful seizure of land, and should an enquiry be held, then the said land shall be returned to the rightful owner thereof, together with the crops sewn, and the fencing, and any buildings:

For these reasons Captain General Troekurov is to be denied the damages he has requested from Lieutenant Dubrovsky, since the estate belonging to him is being restored to his possession, without remainder. And the said estate is to be returned to him in its entirety, no part to be excepted, and should Captain General Troekurov have any clear and legitimate grounds of complaint in this regard, he may therefore lodge a further petition at the appropriate court. This ruling is to be notified in advance to both plaintiff and defendant, together with its foundation in law and procedures for any appeal, plaintiff and defendant to be summoned by the police to this court that they may hear the ruling of the Court and sign in indication of their satisfaction or dissatisfaction.

The secretary finished; the assessor rose and, with a low bow, turned to Troekurov, offering him the document to sign. The triumphant Troekurov took the pen from him and signed the Court's decision, indicating his entire satisfaction.

It was then Dubrovsky's turn. The secretary handed him the document. But Dubrovsky remained motionless, head bowed.

The secretary repeated his invitation to sign, asking Dubrovsky to indicate his complete and entire satisfaction, or his manifest dissatisfaction if, contrary to expectation, feeling in all conscience that his case was just, he intended to appeal within the legally appointed time to the appropriate court... Suddenly Dubrovsky raised his head; his eyes flashed; he stamped his foot, then pushed the secretary out of the way so forcefully that he fell to the ground; seizing the inkwell, he flung it at the assessor. Everyone was appalled. 'What! Have you no respect for the church of the Lord? Out of my way, churls!' Then Dubrovsky turned to Kirila Petrovich: 'It's unheard of, Your Excellency! Kennelmen bringing their dogs into the church of the Lord! Dogs running about the church! I'll teach you!'

Hearing the uproar, the guards rushed in and only with difficulty managed to overpower him. He was led out and put onto his sledge.

Troekurov followed him, accompanied by the entire court. Dubrovsky's sudden madness had made a powerful impression on him and poisoned his triumph.

The judges, who had counted on his gratitude, were not honoured with so much as a single friendly word. Troekurov went straight back to Pokrovskoye. Dubrovsky, meanwhile, lay in bed; the district physician, fortunately not a complete ignoramus, successfully bled him and applied leeches and Spanish fly[1]. Towards evening the sick man began to feel better, and he recovered his senses. The following day he was taken to Kistenevka, which now barely belonged to him.

3

Some time had gone by, but poor Dubrovsky was still not well. True, there were no more fits of madness, but his strength was visibly failing. He forgot his former occupations, rarely left his room and was lost in thought for days on end. He was now being nursed by Yegorovna, a kind-hearted old woman who had at one time looked after his son. She cared for him as if he were a child, reminded him when it was time to eat or sleep, fed him and put him to bed. Andrey Gavrilovich quietly obeyed her and had no contact with anyone else. He was in no state to think about his affairs or take care of his property, and Yegorovna decided she must inform his son, who was then in St Petersburg, serving in one of the regiments of the Foot Guards. And so, tearing out a page from the household accounts book, she dictated a letter to Khariton the cook, the only person in Kistenevka who could read and write, and sent it off to the town to be posted.

But it is time we acquainted the reader with the real hero of our story.

Vladimir Dubrovsky had been educated at the Military Academy and had then joined the Horse Guards with the rank of cornet[2]; his father spared nothing to support him in style, and the young man received more money from home than he had any right to expect. Prodigal and ambitious, he indulged himself in extravagant whims, played cards and ran up debts, not worrying about the future and imagining that sooner or later he would find himself a rich bride – the usual dream of poor young men.

One evening, as several officers sat in his rooms, sprawling on his sofas and smoking his pipes, which had amber mouthpieces, his valet

Grisha handed him a letter. He was immediately struck by the seal and handwriting. He quickly broke the seal and read:

> *Our dear Master Vladimir Andreevich,*
> *I, your old nanny, have resolved to inform you of your Papa's health. He is very poorly, sometimes he wanders in his talk, and he sits there all day like a foolish child – but life and death are in the hands of the Lord. Come home to us soon, light of my eyes, we'll send the horses out to Pesochnoe for you. We have heard the District Court are coming to hand us over to Kirila Petrovich Troekurov, since they say we belong to him, but we have belonged to your family for ever and I have never heard such a thing since the day I was born. You could, living in Petersburg, report this to our father the Tsar, and he won't let us be wronged. I remain your faithful slave and nurse,*
>
> *Orina Yegorovna Byzyreva*
>
> *I send my mother's blessing to Grisha, is he serving you well? It's been raining for over a week now and Rodya the shepherd died close to St Micholas' Day[3].*

Vladimir Dubrovsky read these somewhat confused lines several times with unusual agitation. He had lost his mother in early childhood and had been sent to St Petersburg in his eighth year, barely knowing his father; nevertheless, he felt a romantic attachment to him and he loved family life all the more for never having had the opportunity to enjoy its quiet pleasures.

The thought of losing his father greatly pained his heart, and the condition of this poor sick man, which he surmised from his nurse's letter, filled him with horror. He imagined his father abandoned in a remote village, in the care of a stupid old woman and a few house serfs, threatened by some disaster and fading away, with no one to help him, in torment of body and soul. Vladimir reproached himself for his criminal neglect. It was a long time since he had received any letters from his father and he had not thought of making any enquiries, supposing his father was either travelling somewhere or engrossed in the management of his estate.

He resolved to go and visit him, and even to retire from service should his father's condition require his continued presence. Seeing his anxiety, his comrades went on their way. Vladimir then wrote an application for leave of absence, lit a pipe and sank into deep thought.

He handed in his application later that evening; three days later he was on the highway.

Vladimir Andreevich was nearing the post station where he would be turning off for Kistenevka. His heart was full of sad forebodings; he was afraid of finding his father no longer alive; he was imagining the dismal life awaiting him in the country: a God-forsaken village, loneliness, poverty and struggles to sort out affairs of which he had no understanding. When he reached the post station, he went into the postmaster's office and asked if there were private horses for hire. After enquiring where he was going, the postmaster said that horses from Kistenevka had been waiting for him for over three days. Very soon old Anton the coachman appeared; in the past he had let Vladimir go round the stable with him and had looked after his little pony. At the sight of Vladimir, Anton burst into tears, made a deep bow, said that the old master was still alive, and rushed off to harness the horses. In a hurry to set off, Vladimir refused the meal that was offered to him. Anton drove him along the little country lanes, and the two of them began to talk.

'Please tell me, Anton, what's this I hear about my father and Troekurov?'

'Heaven knows, Master Vladimir Andreevich… Your father, they say, fell foul of Kirila Petrovich, who took him to court, though often enough Kirila Petrovich is his own judge and jury. It's not for us serfs to question our masters, but your father shouldn't have taken on Kirila Petrovich: you can't break an axe with a whip.'

'So this Kirila Petrovich seems to do as he pleases round here?'

'That's the truth, master. He doesn't give a cuss for the assessor, and the police captain's at his beck and call. The gentry gather at his house and they dance attendance on him. As the saying goes: "Set down a trough – and the pigs will come".'

'Is it true he's taking away our estate?'

'Ay, master, that's what we hear tell. Just the other day the sexton from Pokrovskoye says at a christening in our elder's house, "Your good times have come to an end now: Kirila Petrovich will take you in hand good and proper." And Mikita the blacksmith, he answers him, "Enough of that, Savelich, don't go grieving the host and upsetting the guests. Kirila Petrovich is one master, and Andrey Gavrilovich is another master, and every one of us is in the hands of God and the Tsar." But you can't sew buttons on others' mouths.'

'So you don't want to be handed over to Troekurov?'

'Be handed over to Kirila Petrovich! Lord save and preserve us all! His own people often fare badly enough; if he gets his hands on strangers, he'll do worse than skin 'em – he'll tear off their flesh. No, God grant long life to Andrey Gavrilovich, and if the Lord takes him away from us, then we none of us want no master but you, our benefactor. You stand by us, and we'll stand by you!'

Touched by the old coachman's devotion, Dubrovsky fell silent and once again gave himself up to his thoughts. Over an hour went by; he was roused by an exclamation from his valet, Grisha: 'Look – Pokrovskoye!' Dubrovsky looked up. He was on the bank of a broad lake; from it flowed a small river that then wound its way between hills: on one of these hills, above the thick green of trees, could be seen a green roof and the belvedere of a huge stone house; on another hill stood a five-domed church and an old bell-tower; scattered round about were peasant huts with their wells and vegetable plots. Dubrovsky recognised all this: he remembered how he had played on that first hill with little Masha Troekurova, two years younger than him, and promising, even then, to be a beauty. He wanted to ask Anton about her, but some kind of shyness held him back.

As they drew close to the manor-house, he caught a glimpse of a white dress between the trees of the orchard. Just then Anton whipped on the horses and, impelled by the pride common to both country coachmen and city cabbies, rushed full tilt over the bridge and through the village. Leaving the village, they climbed a hill and Vladimir caught sight of a birchwood and, on some open ground to the left, a little grey house with a red roof; his heart beat faster. Before him he could see Kistenevka and his father's sad house.

Ten minutes later he was driving into the courtyard. He looked about him with indescribable emotion. It was twelve years since he had seen his birthplace. What had then been little birch saplings, newly planted beside the fence, had now grown into tall spreading trees. The courtyard, once adorned with three neat flower-beds, a broad carefully swept path running between them, was now an unmowed meadow where a hobbled horse was grazing. The dogs began to bark but, recognising Anton, they fell silent and wagged their shaggy tails. The house serfs all spilled out of their huts and surrounded the young master with loud demonstrations of joy. With difficulty he squeezed through the eager crowd and ran up the dilapidated steps; Yegorovna met him in the entrance-room and wept as she embraced her former charge. 'Greetings, my dear old nurse! Greetings!' he repeated, pressing the kind old woman to his heart. 'And what about Papa? Where's Papa? How is he?'

At that moment, barely able to drag one foot after the other, a tall thin man came into the room; he looked pale and old, and he was wearing a gown and a nightcap.

'Greetings, Volodka!' he said in a weak voice, and Vladimir passionately embraced his father. The invalid's joy was too great a shock for him; he grew faint, his legs gave way under him and, but for his son's support, he would have collapsed.

'Why did you get out of bed?' said Yegorovna. 'You can barely stand – but you still keep trying to be like everyone else!'

The sick man was carried back to his bedroom. He tried to talk to his son, but the thoughts were confused in his head and his speech quite disconnected. He fell silent and dozed off. Vladimir was shaken by his father's condition. He installed himself in his father's bedroom and asked to be left alone with him. The servants obeyed and all turned their attentions to Grisha, leading him to the servants' hall where they welcomed him with the utmost cordiality, feasted him village-style and exhausted him with questions and greetings.

4

Where once was festive fare, now stands a coffin[4]

A few days after his arrival, young Dubrovsky wanted to take up the matter of the estate, but his father was in no condition to provide the necessary explanations; nor was there an attorney. Going through his father's papers, Vladimir found only the assessor's letter and a draft reply; this was not enough to give him any clear understanding of the lawsuit, and he made up his mind to await developments, trusting to the justness of his family's cause.

In the meantime Andrey Gavrilovich's health was worsening by the hour. Vladimir saw that the end was near and never left his side; the old man had now fallen into a state of complete infancy.

Meanwhile the appointed day came and went, and no appeal had been lodged. Kistenevka now belonged to Troekurov. Shabashkin came to visit him, bowing, congratulating him and asking when his High Excellency wished to take possession of his newly acquired property and whether his High Excellency preferred to do this in person or to commission a representative. Kirila Petrovich felt confused. He was not avaricious by nature; his desire for revenge had led him too far; his conscience was murmuring. He knew about the present condition of his adversary, the old comrade of his youth, and victory brought no joy to his heart. He glared at Shabashkin, searching for some reason to give him a good cursing; finding no adequate pretext, he said angrily, 'Not you again. Go away.'

Shabashkin, seeing Troekurov was in a bad mood, bowed and hurried off. Left on his own, Kirila Petrovich began to pace up and down the room, whistling, 'Thunder of Victory, Resound!'[5], always a sign that he was unusually agitated.

In the end he ordered his racing drozhky[6] to be harnessed, put on a warm coat (it was the end of September) and drove out, taking the reins himself.

Soon he could see Andrey Gavrilovich's little house, and his soul was filled by contradictory emotions. Love of power and the satisfaction of vengeance had to some degree stifled his nobler feelings, but the latter finally gained the upper hand. He resolved to make peace with his old neighbour, and to destroy all traces of the quarrel by restoring the property to him. His soul eased by these good intentions, Kirila Petrovich approached his neighbour's house at a trot and drove straight into the yard.

The sick man was sitting at his bedroom window. He recognised Kirila Petrovich and a look of terrible confusion appeared on his face: a purple flush took the place of his usual pallor, his eyes flashed, he uttered unintelligible sounds. Young Dubrovsky, sitting over the household accounts, looked up and felt alarm at the change in his father. The sick man was pointing into the yard with a look of horror and rage. He was hurriedly gathering the folds of his dressing-gown, intending to get up from his chair; he half rose to his feet – and fell. His son rushed over to him; the old man was unconscious and not breathing; he had had a stroke. 'Quick, quick, send for the doctor! Send someone into town!' Vladimir shouted. 'Kirila Petrovich would like to see you,' said a servant in the doorway. Vladimir gave him a terrible look.

'Tell Kirila Petrovich to leave here at once, before I have him thrown out... Now!' The servant rushed from the room, in delight, to carry out his master's command. Yegorovna threw up her hands. 'Dearest master,' she squealed, 'you're bringing ruin down onto your own head! Kirila Petrovich will devour us.' 'Be quiet, nurse,' said Vladimir angrily. 'Send Anton off for a doctor at once.' Yegorovna left the room.

There was no one at all in the vestibule; the servants had all run out to look at Kirila Petrovich. Yegorovna went out onto the porch and heard the servant delivering the young master's answer. Kirila Petrovich listened, still sitting in his drozhky. His face went darker than night; he smiled contemptuously, looked threateningly at the servants and drove slowly round the yard. He glanced at the window where Andrey Gavrilovich had been sitting a minute before, but he was no longer there. The old nurse stood on the porch, forgetting her master's orders. The servants were all holding forth. Suddenly Vladimir appeared in the middle of them and said, 'There's no need for a doctor. Father has died.'

There was confusion. The servants rushed into their old master's room. He was lying in the armchair where Vladimir had carried him; his right hand hung down to the floor, his head lolled on his chest; there was no sign of life in a body still warm but already disfigured by death. Yegorovna let out a wail. The servants surrounded the corpse now left to their care; they washed it, dressed it in a uniform that had been sewn in 1797, and laid it out upon the table their master had sat at for so many years while they had waited upon him.

5

The funeral took place on the third day. The poor old man's body lay on the table, covered by a shroud and surrounded by candles. The dining-room was full of house serfs. They were preparing to carry out the body. Vladimir and three servants lifted the coffin. The priest walked in front; the sexton walked beside him, singing the burial prayers. The master of Kistenevka crossed the threshold of his house for the last time. They carried the coffin through the birchwood; the church lay just beyond it. It was a clear, cold day. Autumn leaves were falling from the trees.

As they left the wood, they saw Kistenevka's wooden church and its cemetery, overshadowed by old lime trees. There lay the body of Vladimir's mother; a fresh pit had been dug beside her grave the evening before.

The church was full of Kistenevka peasants who had come to pay their last respects to their master. Young Dubrovsky stood by the choir; he neither wept nor prayed, but his face was terrifying. The sad rite came to an end. Vladimir went first to say goodbye to the body; he was followed by the house serfs. The lid was brought in and the coffin nailed shut. The women wailed loudly; the men occasionally wiped away tears with their fists. Vladimir and the same three peasants, accompanied by the entire village, carried the coffin to the cemetery. The coffin was lowered into the grave and everyone present threw a handful of sand over it; the pit was filled in; everyone bowed to the grave, then went on their way. Vladimir left quickly, before everyone else, and disappeared into the Kistenevka wood.

Yegorovna, in his name, invited the priest and the rest of the clergy to the funeral dinner, saying that the young master himself would not be present – and so Father Anton, his wife Fedotovna, and the sexton set off for the manor-house, talking with Yegorovna about the virtues of the deceased and the future that, most likely, awaited his heir. Troekurov's visit, and the reception given to him, were already known to the entire neighbourhood, and the local know-alls were predicting serious consequences.

'What will be, will be,' said the priest's wife, 'but I'll be sorry if Vladimir Andreevich isn't to be our landlord. He's a fine fellow, there's no denying it.'

'Who but he can ever be our landlord?' Yegorovna interrupted. 'It's in vain Kirila Petrovich gets himself so heated – my young falcon's not so easily scared. He can stand up for himself, yes, and God willing, his protectors won't abandon him either. And Kirila Petrovich may be terribly high and mighty, but he went off with his tail between his legs all right when my Grishka shouted: "Be off, you old cur! Out of the yard with you!"'

'Mercy on us, Yegorovna!' said the sexton. 'I'm surprised Grigory's tongue didn't refuse to obey him. For my part, I'd sooner lay complaints against the bishop himself than look disrespectfully at Kirila Petrovich. The moment I see him, I'm all bowed down with fear and trembling, and my back just bends and bends and goes on bending.'

'Vanity of vanities,' said the priest. 'One day Eternal Memory will be sung over Kirila Petrovich just as it was sung over Andrey Gavrilovich today. The funeral may be a little grander, and there may be more guests invited back afterwards, but it's all one and the same to God!'

'Oh Father! We wanted to invite the whole neighbourhood, but Vladimir Andreevich refused. We've surely got enough of everything, we wouldn't be put to shame, but what could I do? Well, at least I've put out a nice spread for you, dear guests.'

This cordial invitation and the hope of finding a tasty pie quickened the guests' steps. They soon arrived back at the house, where the table was already laid and the vodka waiting.

Meanwhile Vladimir was deep in the wood, attempting to tire himself out and stifle his sorrow. He walked without thinking where he was going; he kept being caught and scratched by branches, his feet sank into bog, but he noticed nothing. After some time he reached a little hollow, surrounded by forest; a stream wound its way silently beside trees half stripped by autumn. Vladimir stopped; he sat down on the cold turf; thoughts crowded together in his mind, each of them gloomier than the one before. He was overwhelmed by loneliness. Storm clouds hung over his future. The feud with Troekurov held out the promise of new misfortunes. His modest property might be taken away from him, in which case he would be destitute. For a long time he sat in one spot without moving, watching the stream's quiet flow carrying away a few withered leaves – an image of life as true as it was commonplace. Eventually he realised it was growing dark; he got to his feet and began to look for the way home, but he had to wander a long time through unfamiliar parts of the wood before he found the path that led to the gates of his house.

Coming straight towards him were the priest and his party. This was a bad omen, he thought immediately.[7] He involuntarily turned aside and hid behind a tree. No one noticed him, and they carried on talking heatedly as they passed by.

'Keep your distance from evil and do good,' the priest was saying to his wife. 'There's no need for us to hang about. Whatever the outcome, it's not you who's in trouble.' His wife answered, but Vladimir couldn't hear what she said.

As he drew near his house, he saw a large number of people; both peasants and house serfs had crowded into the yard. Even from a distance Vladimir could hear an unusual hubbub. There were two troikas beside the barn. On the porch were several men he didn't know, wearing official uniforms and discussing something.

'What's all this?' he asked angrily, as Anton ran forward to meet him. 'Who are these men? What do they want?'

'Oh my dear master,' the old man answered with a sigh. 'It's officers from the court. They're handing us over to Troekurov, Vladimir Andreevich, they're taking us away from Your Honour!'

Vladimir bowed his head; his serfs surrounded their luckless master. 'You're our father,' they shouted, kissing his hands. 'We don't want no master but you. Just you give the word, sir – we can take care of these here officers. It may be our ruin, but we won't never betray you.' Vladimir looked at them, stirred by unfamiliar feelings. 'Stay where you are,' he said, 'while I speak to the officers.' 'That's right, master, you do that,' shouted voices from the crowd. 'Put the accursed wretches to shame! Have they no conscience?'

Vladimir went up to the officials. Shabashkin, cap on head, stood there with his arms akimbo, looking arrogantly around him. The police captain, a tall stout man of about fifty, with a red face and a moustache, cleared his throat as he saw Dubrovsky coming towards him and pronounced in a hoarse voice: 'And so I repeat what I have already said: by decree of the District Court you now belong to Kirila Petrovich Troekurov, whose person is here represented by Mr Shabashkin. Obey him in all his commands; and you, women, must love and honour him, since he greatly loves you.' The police captain burst out laughing at his witty joke, and Shabashkin and the other officials followed his example. Vladimir was seething with indignation. 'Allow me,' he said with assumed calm, 'to ask what all this means.' 'What this means,' said the witty police captain, 'is that we have come to place Kirila Petrovich Troekurov in possession of this estate and to ask certain others to make themselves scarce while the going's good.' 'But you might, I think, have spoken to me before addressing my peasants, and let a landowner be the first to know that his estate no longer belongs to him…' 'And who might you be?' Shabashkin asked with an insolent look. 'The former landowner, Andrey, son of Gavrila, Dubrovsky, has, by the will of God, passed away. As for you, we neither know you nor wish to know you.'

'Vladimir Andreevich is our young master,' said a voice from the crowd.

'Who was that? Who dared to open his mouth?' asked the police captain threateningly. 'Young master? Vladimir Andreevich? Your master is Kirila Petrovich Troekurov. Got that, blockheads?'

'Not on your life!' said the same voice.

'This is mutiny!' shouted the police captain. 'Hey, where's the village elder?'

The village elder stepped forward.

'Find me that man who just spoke. I'll teach him!'

The elder turned to the crowd and asked who had spoken. But they all remained silent. After a while there were murmurs from the back of the crowd; these grew louder and quickly turned into the most terrible yells. The police captain then softened his voice and tried to calm them down. 'Why are we just gaping at him?' shouted the house serfs. 'Come on, lads, let's send 'em packing!' And the crowd surged forward. Shabashkin and the other officials rushed into the entrance-room and locked the door behind them.

'Come on, let's tie 'em up!' shouted the same voice. And the crowd began to push against the door. 'Stop!' shouted Dubrovsky. 'What are you doing? You'll destroy both yourselves and me. Go back to your homes and leave me in peace. Don't be afraid – the Tsar is merciful and I will appeal to him. He won't let us be wronged. We are all his children. But how can the Tsar intercede on your behalf if you start rioting and behaving like brigands?'

Young Dubrovsky's words, and his resonant voice and commanding air, produced the desired effect. The crowd quietened down and dispersed; the yard emptied. The officials remained in the entrance-room. Finally Shabashkin quietly opened the door, went out onto the porch and, with obsequious bows, began to thank Dubrovsky for his merciful intervention. Vladimir listened to him with contempt and did not answer. 'We have decided,' the assessor continued, 'to remain here, with your permission, for the night. It's dark already, and your peasants might attack us on the road. May I ask you to be so kind as to have some hay spread on the drawing-room floor for us to sleep on? At daybreak, we'll be on our way.'

'Do as you please,' Dubrovsky replied coldly. 'I am no longer master here.' With these words he withdrew into his father's room and locked the door behind him.

6

'So, it's the end of everything,' Vladimir said to himself. 'This morning I had a roof over my head and a crust of bread to eat. Tomorrow I shall be leaving the house where I was born and where my father died, leaving it to the man who killed my father and made a beggar of me.' His eyes came to rest on a portrait of his mother. The painter had depicted her leaning against a balustrade, in a white morning dress and with a red rose in her hair. 'And this portrait too will belong to the enemy of my family,' he said to himself. 'It'll be thrown into a lumber room along with some broken chairs, or else it'll be hung in his vestibule, to be joked about by his kennel-men – and what was once her bedroom, this room where my father just died, will be given over to his steward, or to his harem. No! No! This sad house, from which I am being driven out, shall not belong to Troekurov either.' Vladimir clenched his teeth; terrible thoughts arose in his mind. He could hear the officials: they were lording it up, demanding now this, now that. Their voices were an unwelcome distraction from his sad thoughts. At last, everything fell silent.

Vladimir unlocked chests and drawers and began to go through his late father's papers. For the main part, they consisted of household accounts and business correspondence. Vladimir tore these up without reading them. Among them was a packet with the inscription 'Letters from my Wife'. With deep emotion, Vladimir began reading: the letters had been written at the time of the Turkish campaign[8] and sent to the army from Kistenevka. His mother described her lonely life in the country and her management of the household; she tenderly lamented their long separation and begged her husband to come home, to the embraces of a loving woman. In one letter she expressed anxiety about the health of little Vladimir; in another she rejoiced in his quick development and predicted a brilliant and happy future for him. His soul immersed in a world of family happiness, Vladimir forgot everything else, and he did not notice the passing of time. The wall clock struck eleven. Vladimir put the letters in his pocket, took a candle and left the room. The officials were asleep on the floor of the hall. On the table stood the glasses they had emptied, and the room stank of rum. With a feeling of disgust, Vladimir walked past them into the vestibule. The door to the entrance-room was locked. Not finding the key, he returned to the hall; the key was on the table. Vladimir opened the door and bumped into a man crouching in a corner. An axe gleamed in his hand. Holding the candle towards him, Vladimir recognised Arkhip the blacksmith. 'What are you doing here?' he asked. 'Oh, Vladimir

Andreevich! It's you!' Arkhip whispered back. 'Lord have mercy and save us! It's a good thing you were carrying a candle!' Vladimir looked at him in amazement. 'What are you hiding here for?' he asked the blacksmith.

'I wanted... I came... t-t-to see if the house was still...' Arkhip replied in a quiet stammer.

'And why the axe?'

'The axe? How can I go about at a time like this without an axe? These officials, you know, are scoundrels – you never can tell...'

'You're drunk. Put the axe down, and go and sleep it off.'

'Drunk? Vladimir Andreevich, dear master, God is my witness that not a drop has passed my lips. And how could a man think of vodka at a time like this? Whoever heard of clerks trying to take possession of us, driving our masters off their own property? Listen to them snoring, the accursed wretches! I could do away with the lot of them, and no one the wiser.'

Dubrovsky frowned. 'Listen, Arkhip,' he said, after a brief silence. 'You must put thoughts like that out of your head. It's not the officials who are to blame. Just light your lantern and follow me.'

Arkhip took the candle from his master's hand, found a lantern behind the stove and lit it; the two of them went quietly down the steps and along one side of the yard. Someone on watch began to beat an iron plate; dogs started barking. 'Who's that?' asked Dubrovsky. 'It's us, young master,' answered a thin voice, 'Vasilisa and Lukerya.' 'Go back home,' said Dubrovsky, 'We don't need you here.' 'Have a rest,' added Arkhip. 'Thank you, kind provider,' said the women, and went straight back home.

Dubrovsky walked on. Two men approached; they called out to him. Dubrovsky recognised the voices of Anton and Grisha. 'Why aren't you asleep?' he asked. 'How can we sleep?' replied Anton. 'Who'd have thought it – who'd have thought we'd live to see this?'

'Quiet!' Dubrovsky interrupted. 'Where's Yegorovna?'

'In the main house, in her little attic.'

'Go and fetch her, and get all our people out of the house. See there's not a soul left indoors except the officials. And you, Anton, get a cart ready.'

Grisha went off and reappeared a minute later with his mother. The old woman had not undressed that night; other than the officials, no one in the house had so much as closed an eye.

'Is everyone here?' asked Dubrovsky. 'No one left inside?'

'No one except the clerks,' said Grisha.

'Bring some hay or straw,' said Dubrovsky.

The men ran to the stables and returned with armfuls of hay.

'Put it under the porch. And now, lads, a light!'

Arkhip opened up the lantern. Dubrovsky lit a splinter of wood.

'Wait a moment,' he said to Arkhip. 'I was in such a hurry I think I locked the door into the vestibule. Go and unlock it.'

Arkhip ran in. The door was unlocked. Arkhip locked it, muttering under his breath, 'Unlock it? Not on your life!' – and returned to Dubrovsky.

Dubrovsky put the burning splinter to the hay. The hay caught fire. Flames leapt up, illuminating the courtyard.

'Mercy on us!' wailed Yegorovna. 'Vladimir Andreevich, what are you doing?'

'Quiet!' said Dubrovsky. 'Farewell now, my children. I shall go wherever God leads me. Be happy with your new master.'

'Father and provider,' they all answered. 'We're coming with you. We'd rather die than leave you.'

The horses were led up. Dubrovsky climbed into the cart, along with Grisha, and told the others to meet him in the Kistenevka wood. Anton struck the horses with his whip, and they drove out of the yard.

A wind got up. In a minute the whole house was in flames. Red smoke curled above the roof. Window-panes cracked and fell out; burning beams began to collapse; there were pitiful wails and screams: 'Help, we're burning! Help!' 'Not on your life,' said Arkhip, eyeing the blaze with a malicious smile. 'Arkhipushka,' Yegorovna said to him, 'save the accursed wretches. God will reward you!'

'Not on your life,' said the blacksmith.

The officials appeared at the windows, trying to smash the double frames. But then the roof crashed down, and the screams ceased.

Soon all the domestic serfs were out in the yard. Shouting women were hurrying to save their few possessions; children jumped up and down, admiring the blaze. Sparks flew in a fiery whirlwind; the peasants' huts were catching fire.

'All as it should be,' said Arkhip. 'Burning well, isn't it? A fine sight from Pokrovskoye, I shouldn't wonder.'

Just then something new attracted his attention: a cat was running about on the roof of the blazing barn, not knowing where to jump; it was surrounded on all sides by flame. The poor creature was mewing plaintively for help. Little boys were splitting their sides with laughter as they watched its despair. 'Why are you laughing, you little devils?' said the blacksmith angrily. 'Aren't you afraid of the Lord? One of God's creatures is dying, and you blockheads rejoice.' He placed a ladder against the burning roof and climbed up. The cat understood what he was doing and, with a look of eager gratitude, clutched at his sleeve. The blacksmith, somewhat charred, climbed down with his catch. 'Farewell now, good people,' he said to the bewildered servants. 'There's nothing left for me here. Good luck to you all. Remember me, don't think ill of me.'

The blacksmith went off; the fire continued to rage for some time. Finally it died down; heaps of embers glowed flameless but bright in the darkness; around them wandered Kistenevka's inhabitants, who had lost their all in the blaze.

7

The following day news of the fire spread round the entire neighbourhood. Everyone offered their different guesses and hypotheses. Some made out that Dubrovsky's servants, having got drunk at the funeral, had set fire to the house by mistake; others blamed the officials, saying they had drunk too much as they celebrated taking possession; many maintained that Dubrovsky himself had perished in the fire, along with the court officials and all the servants. Some guessed the truth and asserted that Dubrovsky himself, moved by fury and despair, was to blame for this terrible calamity. Troekurov came round straight away and personally conducted an investigation. It was established that the police captain and the assessor, the scrivener and the clerk of the District Court were all missing, in addition to Vladimir Dubrovsky himself, Yegorovna the old nurse, Anton the coachman, Arkhip the blacksmith and the house serf Grigory. The house serfs all testified that the officials had been burnt to death when the roof fell in; their charred bones were indeed discovered. The servant women Vasilisa and Lukerya said they had seen Dubrovsky and Arkhip the blacksmith a few minutes before the fire. Arkhip the blacksmith, everyone agreed, was still alive and was probably the chief, if not sole, instigator of the fire. But Dubrovsky, too, was under strong suspicion. Kirila Petrovich sent the governor a detailed account of the whole incident, and more legal proceedings began.

It was not long before new reports gave fresh grounds for curiosity and gossip. Brigands appeared, spreading terror throughout the entire district. Measures taken against them by the authorities proved of no avail. Robberies, each more startling than the one before, followed in quick succession. There was no safety either on the roads or in the villages. All over the province, in broad daylight, brigands were driving about in troikas, stopping travellers and mail-coaches, entering villages, pillaging and torching the houses of landowners. The robber chief gained a reputation for intelligence, daring and a certain magnanimity. Wondrous tales were told of him; the name of Dubrovsky was on every lip, everyone being convinced that Dubrovsky was indeed the commander of these daring brigands. Especially astonishing was the fact that Troekurov's estates were being spared; the brigands had not pillaged a single barn or waylaid a single cart that belonged to him. With his usual arrogance, Troekurov put this down to the fear he inspired throughout the province, and also to the exceptionally good police force he had organised in his villages. At first his neighbours joked with one another about Troekurov's presumption, daily expecting uninvited guests to visit Pokrovskoye, an estate where there was certainly plenty for them to loot – but in the end they had no choice but to agree with Troekurov and admit that even brigands treated him with remarkable respect. Troekurov was triumphant; every time he heard about a new exploit of Dubrovsky's, he came out with witticisms about the governor and about the police officers and company commanders from whom Dubrovsky always escaped unharmed.

Meanwhile the 1st of October arrived, the day of the festival – that of Pokrov or the Intercession of the Holy Virgin – after which the church in Troekurov's village was named. But, before we go on to describe this festival and the events that followed it, we must introduce the reader to characters who are either new to him or else have been mentioned only briefly at the beginning of our tale.

8

The reader, most probably, has already guessed that Kirila Petrovich's daughter, about whom we have so far said only a few words, is the heroine of our tale. At the time of which we are writing she was seventeen and in the full flower of her beauty. Her father loved her to distraction but treated her in his usual capricious manner, one moment attempting to indulge every least whim of hers, another moment frightening her with his sternness, and sometimes even cruelty. Confident as he was of her affection, he was unable to win her trust. She had grown used to hiding her thoughts and feelings from him, since she never knew how he would respond. She had no friends and had grown up in solitude. The neighbours' wives and daughters seldom visited Kirila Petrovich, whose usual conversation and amusements called more for masculine bonhomie than the presence of ladies. Seldom did our young beauty appear among the guests feasting with Kirila Petrovich. The huge library, consisting mainly of the works of French writers of the eighteenth century, had been placed at her disposal. Her father, who never read anything except *The Ideal Cook*, was unable to guide her in her choice of books, and Masha, after dipping into works of every genre, naturally ended up reading novels. Thus she completed the education begun some time ago by Mlle Mimi, a woman whom Kirila Petrovich had trusted and greatly liked and whom he had been obliged to send off discreetly to another of his estates when the consequences of his friendship with her eventually became too apparent. People had fond memories of Mlle Mimi. She was a good-hearted girl and – unlike the other mistresses who replaced one another in quick succession – she had never abused the influence she clearly had on Kirila Petrovich. Kirila Petrovich seemed to have loved her more than the others, and a naughty, dark-eyed little nine-year-old boy, whose southern features recalled those of Mlle Mimi, was being brought up in the house as his son, even though a great many other little boys, as like Kirila Petrovich as one drop of water to another, ran about barefoot outside his windows and were regarded as serf-children. Kirila Petrovich had ordered a French tutor to be sent down from Moscow for his little Sasha, and this tutor arrived at the time of the events we are now describing.

The tutor's pleasant appearance and straightforward manner made a favourable impression on Kirila Petrovich. He presented his testimonials, together with a letter from a relative of Troekurov's at whose house he had served as a tutor for four years. Kirila Petrovich examined everything and was dissatisfied only with the Frenchman's youth – not because he thought this likeable shortcoming indicated a lack of the patience and experience so necessary to anyone in the unfortunate role of tutor, but because he had other doubts, which he resolved to voice to the young man at once. To this end he sent for Masha (Kirila Petrovich did not speak French, and she acted as his interpreter).

'Come here, Masha. Tell this moosieur that yes, I'll take him on, but only on condition he doesn't start chasing after my girls. Or I'll teach him, the son of a bitch… Translate that, Masha.'

Masha blushed and, turning to the tutor, said to him in French that her father counted on his modest and proper conduct.

The Frenchman bowed to her and replied that he hoped to earn respect even if he did not win favour.

Masha translated his reply word for word.

'Very good, very good,' said Kirila Petrovich. 'But he needn't be bothering himself about either favour or respect. His business is to look after Sasha and to teach him grammar and geography. Translate that to him.'

Maria Kirilovna softened her father's rudeness in her translation, and Kirila Petrovich dismissed the Frenchman, ordering him to be shown to the wing where a room had been prepared for him.

Masha paid no attention to the young Frenchman: brought up

with the prejudices of an aristocrat, she looked on a tutor as a kind of servant or artisan – and a servant or artisan, in her eyes, was not a man. She noticed neither the general impression she made on M. Desforges, nor his embarrassment, nor his agitation, nor the change in his voice. Several days in a row she came across him fairly often, but without taking any particular notice of him. An unexpected incident showed him in a new light.

There were usually a number of bear cubs being raised in one of the yards; these were one of the chief amusements of the master of Pokrovskoye. When they were very little, they were brought every day into the living-room and Kirila Petrovich would play with them for hours on end, setting them against the cats and puppies. When they grew up, they were put on a chain, to await being baited in earnest. Sometimes they were led out in front of the windows of the main house and an empty wine cask studded with nails was rolled towards them; the bear would sniff the cask, touch it cautiously, and hurt its paw; angered, it would push the cask more violently and hurt itself still more. Then it would work itself into a perfect frenzy, growling and flinging itself at the barrel until the object of the poor beast's futile rage was taken away. On other occasions a pair of bears was harnessed to a cart, and visitors, willing or unwilling, were seated in it and sent off who knows where at a gallop. But Kirila Petrovich's favourite prank was the following.

A hungry bear would be locked in an empty room, tethered by a rope to a ring in the wall. The rope ran almost the length of the room, so that only the furthest corner was safe from the attacks of the terrible beast. Some novice would be led to the door of the room, pushed in and locked inside; the unfortunate victim was then left on his own with the shaggy recluse. The poor visitor, scratched and bleeding, his coat ripped, would quickly discover the safe corner, but he would sometimes have to stand there as long as three hours, flattening himself against the wall while the furious beast, only a couple of steps away, leapt, growled, got up on its hind legs and vainly struggled to claw him. Such were the noble pastimes of a Russian gentleman!

A few mornings after the tutor's arrival, Troekurov took it into his head to entertain him, too, with a visit to the bear's room. He sent for him, then led him down some dark corridors; a side door opened, and two servants instantly pushed the Frenchman in and locked the door after him. Recovering from his surprise, the tutor saw the tethered bear; the animal snorted, sniffed from a distance at its visitor and, standing up on its hind legs, advanced on him. The Frenchman, unruffled, stood his ground and awaited the attack. The bear came close; Desforges took a small pistol from his pocket, held it to the hungry beast's ear, and fired. The bear rolled over. Everyone came running, the door opened, and Kirila Petrovich came in, astonished at this unexpected denouement to his joke. He insistently demanded an explanation: who had alerted Desforges to the joke about to be played on him? Or what other reason did he have for carrying a loaded pistol in his pocket? He sent for Masha. Masha hurried in and translated her father's questions to the Frenchman.

'I knew nothing of the bear,' Desforges replied, 'but I always carry a pistol about my person, because I do not intend to endure insults for which, in view of my position, I am unable to demand satisfaction.'

Masha looked at him in amazement and translated his words to Kirila Petrovich. Kirila Petrovich made no answer, ordered the bear to be taken out and skinned, then turned to his men and said, 'What a fine fellow! He's certainly no coward. No sir!' From that moment he felt a fondness for Desforges, and he never again thought of putting him to the test.

The incident made a still deeper impression on Maria Kirilovna. Her imagination was enthralled: in her mind's eye she kept seeing the dead bear, and Desforges standing calmly over the bear and calmly conversing with her. She realised that courage and a sense of proper pride were not the exclusive attribute of a single class, and from then on she began to show the young tutor a respect that included more and more warmth of feeling. A certain intimacy arose between them. Masha had a fine voice and great musical ability; Desforges offered to give her lessons. After this, it will be easy enough for the reader to guess that Masha fell in love with him, not yet acknowledging this even to herself.

Volume Two

9

The guests began to arrive on the eve of the feast-day. Some stayed in the manor-house or its wings, some at the steward's, some at the priest's, and others with the more well-to-do peasants. The stables were full of horses, the yards and barns packed with all kinds of carriages. At nine in the morning the bells began to ring for Mass and everyone set off for the new stone church that Kirila Petrovich had had built and that he embellished with new gifts every year. There was such a crowd of distinguished worshippers that there was no room for anyone else, and the ordinary peasants had to stand on the porch or in the churchyard. Mass had not yet begun; they were waiting for Kirila Petrovich. He arrived in a coach-and-six and solemnly walked to his place, accompanied by Maria Kirilovna. The eyes of both men and women were turned on her – the men marvelling at her beauty and the women scrutinising her dress. The mass began. The choir was formed from Kirila Petrovich's house serfs, and he himself joined in with them; he prayed, looking neither to left nor to right, and he bowed to the ground with proud humility when the deacon spoke, in a voice as loud as thunder, of the founder of this church.

The mass came to an end. Kirila Petrovich was first to go up and kiss the cross. Everyone else did the same. Kirila Petrovich's neighbours then paid their respects to him. The ladies surrounded Masha. As he left the church, Kirila Petrovich invited everyone to dine with him; he got into his carriage and set off home. Everyone drove off after him.

Kirila Petrovich's rooms were filling with guests. Every minute new people arrived and could barely push their way through to the master of the house. The ladies sat in a decorous semicircle, all in pearls and diamonds, dressed in costly old-fashioned gowns that had seen better days; the men crowded round the vodka and caviar, raising their voices as they talked and argued with one another. The table in the dining-hall had been laid for eighty. The house serfs bustled about, arranging bottles and decanters and straightening tablecloths. At last the butler announced 'Dinner is served', and Kirila Petrovich was first to take his place at the table. The ladies followed him and solemnly took their places, according to their respective ages; the young girls huddled together like a timid flock of kid goats, making sure they could all sit next to one another. The men sat down opposite. At the end of the table, beside little Sasha, sat the tutor.

The house serfs began to serve the guests, according to rank; when they were uncertain, they followed the principles of Lavater and hardly made a mistake.[9] The clink of plates and spoons mingled with the loud voices of the guests. Kirila Petrovich looked round the table merrily, enjoying to the full the happiness of playing the hospitable host. Just then a coach-and-six drew into the yard. 'Who's that?' asked the host. 'Anton Pafnutich,' answered several voices. The door opened and Anton Pafnutich Spitsyn, a stout man of about fifty with a round pock-marked face adorned by a triple chin, burst into the dining-room, bowing, smiling, and already preparing his apologies. 'Set a place for him right here,' shouted Kirila Petrovich. 'Welcome, Anton Pafnutich! Sit down and tell us the meaning of all this: you missed my Mass and now you're late for dinner. It's not like you at all: you're a pious man and you're fond of your food.' 'I'm sorry,' Anton Pafnutich replied, tucking a corner of his napkin into a buttonhole of his pea-green kaftan[10]. 'Excuse me, dear sir Kirila Petrovich. I set off in good time but I'd barely gone five miles when the rim of one of my front wheels split in half – what could I do? Fortunately we weren't far from a village, but it still took us three whole hours to drag the carriage there, track down the blacksmith and patch things up as best we could. There was nothing for it. And I didn't dare take the short cut across Kistenevka wood – I took the roundabout way.'

'Oho!' Kirila Petrovich broke in, 'I can see you're no hero! And what is it you're so afraid of?'

'What is it I'm afraid of, dear sir Kirila Petrovich? Why, I'm afraid of Dubrovsky! Who knows when one might not fall into his clutches? He's nobody's fool and he doesn't let people off lightly. As for me, he'd skin me twice over.'

'And what, brother, might make him single you out for such an honour?'

'What do you mean, dear sir Kirila Petrovich? Because of the lawsuit against the late Andrey Gavrilovich! Wasn't it I who, for your own satisfaction – that is in accord with truth and my conscience – testified that the Dubrovskys had no right to the property, and were living in Kistenevka only by virtue of your own generosity? The late Andrey Gavrilovich (may he rest in peace) said he'd get even with me one way or another; might not the son keep his father's word? Until now, God has spared me. So far they've only pillaged one of my barns, but who knows when they might not plunder the house?'

'They'll have a fine time when they do,' said Kirila Petrovich. 'Your little red-leather coffer must be crammed to the brim.'

'What do you mean, my dear sir Kirila Petrovich? It was once, but now it's quite empty.'

'Enough of your humbug, Anton Pafnutich! We all know what you're like: what do you ever spend money on? You live like a pig in a sty, you don't receive guests, you fleece your peasants – I'll vow you've been putting away a tidy sum!'

'You are pleased to joke, dear sir Kirila Petrovich,' Anton Pafnutich murmured with a smile, 'but I swear to you that we're ruined.' He then took away the taste of his host's high-handed jokes with a slice of rich pie. Kirila Petrovich decided to let him be; he turned his attention to the new police captain, who had come to the house for the first time and was sitting at the far end of the table, beside the tutor.

'Well, Mister Captain, are you going to be catching Dubrovsky for us?'

Thrown into a panic, the captain bowed, smiled, stammered and finally brought out the words: 'We'll do our best, Your Excellency.'

'Your best, eh? You people have been doing your best for some time now, but not much has come of it yet. But then, why should you want to catch him? Dubrovsky's robberies are a godsend for a police captain: journeys, investigations, expeditions – yes, it all helps feather the nest. Why do away with such a benefactor? Isn't that so, Mister Captain?'

'That's the absolute truth, Your Excellency,' said the police captain, totally confused.

The guests all roared with laughter.

'I like the young fellow's honesty,' said Kirila Petrovich, 'but it's a pity about our late captain Taras Alekseevich. Yes, if he hadn't been in the fire, it would be a lot quieter in these parts. But what news of Dubrovsky? When was he last seen?'

'At my house, Kirila Petrovich,' came a lady's deep voice. 'He dined with me last Tuesday.'

All eyes turned towards Anna Savishna Globova, a widow whom everyone loved for her straightforward, kind and cheerful disposition. The party awaited her story with interest.

'Well, three weeks ago I sent my steward to the post with some money for my young Vanya. I don't spoil my son, and I'm in no position to spoil him even if I wanted to, but, as you all know, an officer in the Guards has to look after himself properly and I share with my Vanya what little income I have. And so I sent him two thousand roubles. The thought of Dubrovsky did cross my mind, but I said to myself: it's not far to the town, only five miles; with God's help the money will get through. And then, come evening – my steward returns on foot, pale-faced and with his clothes all torn. "What's the matter?" I gasp. "What's happened to you?" "Dear ma'am Anna Savishna," he says, "highwaymen robbed me. They nearly killed me. Dubrovsky was one of them; he wanted to hang me, but then he took pity on me and let me go – but not without taking everything I had, even the horse and cart." My heart almost stopped: Father in heaven, what'll become of my Vanya? But what could I do? I wrote my son another letter; I told him everything and sent him my blessing, without so much as a kopek.

'A week went by, then another week – suddenly a carriage drives into my yard. Some general's asking to see me; I invite him in. In comes a man of about thirty-five, swarthy, black-haired, a moustache and beard, the spitting image of Kulnev[11]. He introduces himself as a friend and comrade of my late husband Ivan Andreevich; he was driving past and, knowing I live here, he couldn't not call on his old comrade's widow. I treated him to what food I had in the house; we talked about this and that, and in the end we got to Dubrovsky. "That's very strange," he said. "What I've heard is that Dubrovsky doesn't attack just anyone but only people generally known to be wealthy – and that he's merciful even to them and never strips them of everything. And no one's ever accused him of murder. I wonder if there hasn't been some mischief – pray send for your steward." I sent for the steward. The man came in; seeing the general, he was dumbfounded. "So tell me, my good fellow, the story of how Dubrovsky robbed you and wanted to hang you." My steward began to tremble, and he threw himself at the general's feet. "Gracious sir, I did wrong – it was the work of the devil – I lied." "In that case," said the general, "be so kind as to tell the lady just what did happen, and I shall listen." My steward was speechless. "Come on," said the general, "tell us where you met Dubrovsky!" "By the two pines, gracious sir, by the two pines." "And what did he say to you?" "He asked me whose man I was, where was I going, and why." "And after that?" "After that he demanded the letter and the money." "And then?" "Then I gave him the letter and the money." "And then? What did he do then?" "Gracious sir, I did wrong." "But what did Dubrovsky do?" "He returned the money and the letter, and he said, 'Well, God be with you. Take it to the post.'" "And what did you do?" "Gracious sir, I did wrong." "I'll settle with you later, my dear friend," said the general menacingly. "And you, madam, should first order this scoundrel's trunk to be searched, then hand him over to me so I can teach him a lesson. I'd like you to know that Dubrovsky was once an officer in the Guards himself and it's not like him to do wrong to a comrade." Well, I had some idea who His Excellency really was, but I thought it was best to keep mum. His coachmen tied the steward to the box of the carriage. They found the money; the general had dinner with me and went off straight afterwards, taking the steward with him. The steward was found in the forest the next day, tied to an oak and flogged good and proper.'

The entire company, and especially the young ladies, listened to Anna Savishna's story with bated breath. Many of them secretly wished Dubrovsky well, seeing him as a romantic hero; this was especially true of Maria Kirilovna, an ardent dreamer who had been brought up on the mysterious horrors of Mrs Radcliffe.

'And so you imagine that was Dubrovsky, Anna Savishna?' asked Kirila Petrovich. 'You're very mistaken. I don't know who your visitor was, but it certainly wasn't Dubrovsky.'

'What do you mean, my dear sir? Who else but Dubrovsky roams the highways, stopping travellers and searching them?'

'I've no idea, but your visitor certainly wasn't Dubrovsky. I can remember him as a child. His hair may have gone dark since, though it was fair and curly when he was little – but I know for sure that

Dubrovsky is five years older than my Masha, and that makes him not thirty-five but around twenty-three.'

'Exactly so, Your Excellency,' observed the police captain. 'I have a description of Vladimir Dubrovsky in my pocket. It says quite precisely that he's in his twenty-third year.'

'Ah!' said Kirila Petrovich. 'There's an idea. Perhaps you could read us that description. It would be no bad thing if we all knew his distinguishing features. If we happen to run into him, we wouldn't want him slipping away, would we?'

The captain took a rather dirty sheet of paper from his pocket, solemnly unfolded it, and read in a singsong voice: 'Distinguishing features of Vladimir Dubrovsky, based upon descriptions given by his former serfs. Age: twenty-two years. Height: medium. Complexion: clear. Beard: none. Eyes: brown. Hair: light brown. Nose: straight. Special distinguishing features: none.'

'That's all?' asked Kirila Petrovich.

'That's all,' replied the captain, folding the paper.

'My congratulations, Mister Captain. That's quite a document! With distinguishing features like that you'll have no trouble finding Dubrovsky. After all, there aren't so many people of medium height, with light brown hair, a straight nose and brown eyes! I'll wager you could talk three full hours with Dubrovsky himself and not realise whom Fate has thrown in your path. There's no denying it, you officers are a smart lot!'

The captain meekly put the document back in his pocket and turned silently to his goose and cabbage. Meanwhile, the servants had been round the table several times, refilling everyone's glasses. Several bottles of Caucasian and Crimean wine had been loudly uncorked and favourably received under the name of champagne; faces were beginning to glow; conversations were becoming louder, merrier and less coherent.

'No,' Kirila Petrovich went on, 'we'll never see another captain like the late Taras Alekseevich! He knew what was what, no one could pull the wool over his eyes. A pity he was burnt in the fire – not one of this band would have escaped a man like him. He'd have caught every last one of them; not even Dubrovsky himself could have wriggled or bribed his way out. Taras Alekseevich would have accepted his bribe all right, but he wouldn't have let him go. Yes, that was the way of the deceased. Well, there's nothing for it – seems I'll have to take the law into my own hands and go after the brigands with my own men. I'll begin by detailing twenty men to scour the robbers' wood. My men aren't cowards, every one of them would take on a bear single-handed, they're not the sort to run from robbers.'

'How is your bear, dear sir Kirila Petrovich?' asked Anton Pafnutich, reminded by these words of his shaggy acquaintance and of certain jests of which he had once been the victim. 'Misha has departed this life,' replied Kirila Petrovich. 'He died a glorious death, at the hands of the enemy. There sits his conqueror.' And Kirila Petrovich pointed at Desforges. 'You should commission a portrait of my Frenchman. He has avenged your... begging your pardon. Do you remember?'

'How could I not remember?' said Anton Pafnutich, scratching himself. 'I remember very well. So Misha's dead, I'm sorry, upon my word I'm sorry! What a joker he was! How quick-witted! You'll never find another bear like him. And why did moosieur kill him?'

Kirila Petrovich began with great pleasure to relate the bold deed carried out by his Frenchman, for he possessed the fortunate ability to take pride in everything around him. The guests listened attentively to the tale of Misha's death and looked with amazement at Desforges, who, not suspecting that the subject of the conversation was his own bravery, was sitting quietly at the table, now and again admonishing his restive pupil.

The dinner, which had lasted about three hours, came to an end. The host put his napkin on the table, and everyone got to their feet and went to the drawing-room, where coffee and cards awaited them, and a continuation of the drinking so splendidly begun in the dining-hall.

10

Around seven in the evening some of the guests wanted to go but the host, merry from punch, ordered the gates to be locked and declared that no one would be allowed to leave the house until morning. Soon afterwards the band struck up, the doors to the hall were opened and dancing began. The host and his cronies sat in one corner, drinking glass after glass and delighting in the gaiety of the young. The old women played cards. As always, except where some cavalry brigade is quartered, there were fewer gentlemen than ladies, and every man fit to dance was recruited. The tutor especially distinguished himself: he danced more than anyone, all the young ladies choosing him and finding him extremely easy to waltz with. He whirled round several times with Maria Kirilovna, and the other young ladies made little jokes as they watched. At last, around midnight, the tired host brought the dancing to an end, ordered supper to be served and himself retired to bed.

With Kirila Petrovich out of the way, the guests felt more at ease and more animated. Gentlemen ventured to sit next to ladies. The young girls laughed and exchanged whispers with their neighbours; the ladies talked loudly across the table. The men drank, argued and roared with laughter – in short, it was an extremely enjoyable meal that left behind many a pleasant memory.

Only one person did not share in the general merriment: Anton Pafnutich sat there gloomy and silent, eating abstractedly and looking extremely anxious. The talk of brigands had troubled his imagination. We shall soon see that he had reason enough to fear them.

In calling God to witness that his little red-leather coffer was empty, Anton Pafnutich had not lied or sinned: his little coffer was indeed empty, the money he kept in it having been transferred to a leather pouch he wore against his chest, beneath his shirt. Only through this precaution was he able to calm his constant fearfulness and his mistrust of everyone around him. Obliged to spend the night in someone else's house, he was afraid of being assigned some remote room that could easily be broken into by thieves. He looked around for a reliable companion, and in the end he chose Desforges. Desforges' obvious physical strength and – still more – the courage he had shown on encountering the bear, whom poor Anton Pafnutich was himself unable to remember without trembling, decided his choice. When they got up from the table, Anton Pafnutich began circling about near the young Frenchman, coughing and clearing his throat; in the end he turned to him with this request:

'Hm, hm, could I possibly, moosieur, spend the night in your little room, because, you see…'

'*Que désire Monsieur?*'[12] asked Desforges, bowing politely.

'Oh how unfortunate it is, moosieur, that you have not yet learnt Russian. *Je veux, moi, chez vous coucher.*[13] Do you understand?'

'*Monsieur, très volontiers,*' said Desforges. '*Veuillez donner des ordres en conséquence.*'[14]

Very pleased with his fluency in the French tongue, Anton Pafnutich went off at once to tell the servants.

The guests began wishing one another goodnight and retiring to their appointed rooms; Anton Pafnutich and the tutor went across to the wing. It was a dark night. Desforges lit the way with a lantern; Anton Pafnutich walked behind in fairly good spirits, occasionally pressing his secret pouch to his breast to check that his money was still there.

When they reached the room, the tutor lit a candle and they undressed. At the same time, Anton Pafnutich paced around, checking the locks and windows and shaking his head, disheartened by what he found. The door was closed only by a latch, and the windows had not yet been fitted with their second frames. He tried to complain about this to Desforges, but his knowledge of the French tongue proved inadequate for a discussion of such complex matters; the Frenchman did not understand him and Anton Pafnutich had no choice but to stop complaining. The two beds were opposite one another; the men lay down, and the tutor blew out the candle.

'*Pourquoi vous touchez, pourquoi vous touchez?*' Anton Pafnutich called out, doing his best to conjugate the Russian for 'to extinguish' as if it were a French verb. 'I cannot *dormir* in the dark.' Not understanding his exclamations, Desforges wished him goodnight.

'Damned heathen!' muttered Anton Pafnutich, wrapping himself in his blanket. 'Why does he have to go and blow out the candle? How's that going to help him?' 'Moosieur, moosieur,' he went on, *'je veux avec vous parler'*.[15] But the Frenchman said nothing and soon began to snore.

'Snoring brute of a Frenchman!' thought Anton Pafnutich. 'I'll be lucky if I get any sleep at all myself. Any moment now thieves will walk in through an unlocked door, or they'll climb through the window – and not even a cannon's going to wake this brute!'

'Moosieur! Moosieur! The devil take you!'

Anton Pafnutich fell silent; fatigue and the effects of alcohol gradually got the better of his fearfulness. He dozed off and soon sank into deep slumber.

A strange awakening was in store for him. Still asleep, he felt that someone was gently pulling at his shirt collar. Anton Pafnutich opened his eyes and saw Desforges standing over him in the pale light of an autumn morning: the Frenchman was holding a pocket pistol in one hand and unfastening the precious pouch with the other. Anton Pafnutich's heart stood still.

'Qu'est-ce que c'est, moosieur, qu'est-ce que c'est?'[16] he brought out in a trembling voice.

'Sssh! Be quiet!' the tutor replied in the purest Russian. 'Be quiet, or you're done for. I am Dubrovsky.'

11

We shall now ask the reader of our tale for permission to explain these last events by certain previous incidents that we have not yet had time to relate.

In a corner of the post-station building whose postmaster we have already mentioned, there sat a traveller whose meek, patient air showed him to be either a member of the intelligentsia or a foreigner – a man, anyway, who had no rights at post-stations. His trap stood outside in the yard, waiting for grease for its wheels. In it lay a small suitcase, proof of his restricted circumstances. The traveller asked for neither tea nor coffee but just looked through the window and whistled – to the great displeasure of the postmaster's wife, who was sitting behind the partition.

'So the Lord's sent us a whistler,' she said, under her breath. 'May he be struck dumb, the damned infidel!'

'Why?' asked the postmaster. 'Where's the harm in it? Let him whistle!'

'The harm in it?' his wife repeated crossly. 'Don't you know the saying?'

'What saying? That whistling blows away money? No, Pakhomovna, it makes no difference to us. There's no money here to be blown away.'

'Send him on his way, Sidorych. What are you keeping him for? Give him some horses and let him go to the devil.'

'He can wait, Pakhomovna. I've only three troikas in the stables; the fourth is resting. Who knows – some better traveller may turn up. No, I'm not risking my neck for a Frenchman. Ha! What did I say? Here's one right now. Aha! And at a gallop! Could be a general!'

A carriage stopped by the porch. A servant jumped down from the box and opened the door, and a moment later a young man in a military greatcoat and a white cap came in; the servant followed, bringing a small box which he placed on the window-sill.

'Horses!' said the officer imperiously.

'At once,' said the postmaster. 'May I have your travelling papers?'

'I don't have any. I'm not taking the main road. Do you not recognise me?'

The postmaster bustled around and rushed out to hurry up the coachmen. The young man paced up and down the room, then went behind the partition and quietly asked the postmaster's wife who the other traveller was.

'God only knows,' she replied. 'Some Frenchman or other. Five hours now he's been waiting for horses and whistling. I've had enough of the wretch.'

The young man began to talk to the traveller in French.

'May I ask where you are going?' he asked.

'To the nearest town,' the Frenchman replied, 'and from there to a landowner who's engaged me by letter as a tutor. I thought I'd be there today, but Monsieur Postmaster seems to have decided otherwise. It's not so easy to get horses in this country, Monsieur Officer.'

'And which of the local landowners are you going to be working for?' asked the officer.

'Monsieur Troekurov.'

'Troekurov? What kind of a man is this Troekurov?'

'*Ma foi, mon officier*,[17] I've not heard much good of him. They say he's a proud and headstrong gentleman and that he treats his subordinates cruelly. No one can get on with him, everyone trembles at the mere mention of his name, and he doesn't stand upon ceremony with tutors. He's already flogged two to death.'

'Heaven help us! And you're resolved to work for a monster like that?'

'What can I do, Monsieur Officer? He's offering me a good salary – three thousand roubles a year, with board and lodging. Maybe I'll be luckier than the others. My mother's an old woman; I'll be sending off half my salary for her to live on, and within five years I'll have saved enough from the other half to secure my independence. Then, *bonsoir* – I'll be off to Paris to set myself up in business.'

'Does anyone in Troekurov's house know you?'

'No,' said the tutor. 'He heard of me through a friend of his in Moscow, whose cook, a compatriot of mine, recommended me. I should say that I first intended to work not as a tutor but as a pastry-chef, but I was told that in your country the calling of tutor is a great deal more profitable.'

The officer stood thinking.

'Listen,' he said, 'how would you feel if, instead of this position, someone offered you ten thousand roubles in cash on condition you return at once to Paris?'

The Frenchman looked at the officer in amazement, smiled, and shook his head.

'Your horses are ready,' said the postmaster, coming into the room. The servant repeated this.

'Thank you,' said the officer. 'Leave the room for a moment.' The postmaster and the servant both left. 'I'm not joking,' he continued in French. 'I can give you ten thousand roubles. In return I ask only for your absence and your papers.' With these words he opened his box and took out several bundles of banknotes.

The Frenchman gaped. He didn't know what to think.

'My absence… my papers,' he repeated in amazement. 'Here are my papers… But you're joking. What use are my papers to you?'

'That's no concern of yours. I'm asking you: do you agree, or not?'

The Frenchman, still unable to believe his ears, handed his papers to the young officer, who quickly looked through them.

'Your passport… Good. Letter of recommendation, let me see. Birth certificate, splendid. Here's your money then – you can go back home. Goodbye.'

The Frenchman stood rooted to the spot.

The officer came back.

'I almost forgot the most important thing. Give me your word of honour that all this will remain between ourselves. Your word of honour.'

'My word of honour,' the Frenchman replied. 'But what about my papers? How will I get by without them?'

'Report in the first town you come to that you were robbed by Dubrovsky. The authorities will believe you and give you the necessary attestation. Goodbye. God grant you return quickly to Paris and find your mother in good health.'

Dubrovsky left the room, got into his carriage and galloped off.

The postmaster looked out of the window and, when the carriage was out of sight, he turned to his wife with the exclamation, 'You know what, Pakhomovna? That was Dubrovsky!'

The postmistress rushed to the window, but it was too late: Dubrovsky was far away. She began scolding her husband:

'Have you no fear of the Lord, Sidorych? Why didn't you tell me before? I could have caught a glimpse of Dubrovsky! He won't be back now till kingdom come. Shameless, that's what I call you, shameless!'

The Frenchman still stood rooted to the spot. His agreement with the officer, the money – it all seemed like a dream. But the bundles of banknotes were there in his pocket, eloquently confirming the truth of this astonishing event.

He made up his mind to hire horses to the nearest town. The coachman drove at a slow pace, and night fell before they arrived.

Before reaching the town gate, where there was a tumbledown sentry-box but no sentry, the Frenchman ordered the driver to stop, got out of the trap, and continued on foot, explaining through gestures that the driver was to keep the trap and the suitcase by way of a tip. The driver was as much astonished by such generosity as the Frenchman himself had been by Dubrovsky's proposal. But, concluding that the dumb foreigner had gone out of his mind, he thanked him with a low bow and, considering it wiser not to enter the town, he made his way to a certain house of entertainment, whose landlord he knew exceedingly well. There he spent the entire night; in the morning he set off back home with the three horses but no trap and no suitcase; he had a swollen face and red eyes.

Having obtained the Frenchman's papers, Dubrovsky boldly presented himself, as we have seen, to Troekurov and settled into his house. Whatever his secret intentions (and we shall learn these in due course), his conduct was blameless. True, he did not greatly concern himself with little Sasha's education. He gave the boy free rein, letting him get up to all kinds of mischief, and he was far from exacting with regard to lessons, which he set only to keep up appearances; he did, however, devote himself with great diligence to the musical progress of his other pupil, often sitting with her at the piano for hours on end. Everybody loved the young tutor: Kirila Petrovich – for his quick daring when they were out hunting; Maria Kirilovna – for his boundless zeal and timid attentiveness; Sasha – for treating him with indulgence when he got up to mischief; the servants – for his kindness and for a generosity which seemed out of keeping with his position. He himself seemed to have grown attached to the whole family and to consider himself one of its members.

About a month had gone by between his taking up the calling of tutor and the festivities we have described – and no one suspected that the modest young Frenchman might really be the terrible brigand whose name alone was enough to inspire terror in all the local landowners. Dubrovsky had not once left Pokrovskoye, but rumours about his robberies continued to spread, thanks to the inventive imagination of those who dwell in the country; though it may also have been that his band continued their activities even in the absence of their chief.

Passing the night in the same room as a man whom he had reason to consider his personal enemy and one of the principal authors of his misfortunes, Dubrovsky was unable to resist temptation. He knew about the existence of the pouch and he decided to gain possession of it. We have seen how he amazed poor Anton Pafnutich by his sudden transformation from tutor to brigand.

At nine o'clock in the morning, the guests who had passed the night at Pokrovskoye began to gather one after another in the drawing-room, where a samovar was already boiling; seated before it was Maria Kirilovna in her morning dress, while Kirila Petrovich, in a flannelette frock-coat and slippers, was drinking tea from a cup as broad as a slop-basin. The last to appear was Anton Pafnutich; he was so pale and seemed so distressed that everyone was startled by the mere sight of him and Kirila Petrovich enquired after his health. Anton Pafnutich answered incoherently and kept looking in horror at the tutor, who was sitting there as if nothing had happened. A few minutes later a servant came in and announced that Anton Pafnutich's carriage was ready; he hurried to take his leave and, in spite of his host's protestations, rushed out of the room and drove off straight away. No one could understand what was the matter with him, and Kirila Petrovich decided he had overeaten. After morning tea and a farewell luncheon, the other guests began to disperse; soon Pokrovskoye was empty and everything resumed its normal course.

12

Several days passed, and nothing worthy of note occurred. Life at Pokrovskoye was the same as ever. Kirila Petrovich went out hunting every day, while Maria Kirilovna kept herself occupied with reading, going for walks and – most important of all – music lessons. She was beginning to understand her own heart and, with involuntary irritation, to acknowledge that it was not indifferent to the fine qualities of the young Frenchman. He for his part never stepped beyond the bounds of respect and strict propriety, thus soothing her pride and timorous doubts. She surrendered ever more trustingly to a captivating routine.

She felt listless without Desforges; and when they were together, she gave him her full attention, wanting to know his opinion about everything and always agreeing with him. She may not yet have been in love, but it was evident that, at the first chance obstacle or vicissitude of fate, the flame of passion would flare up in her heart.

One day Maria went into the hall, where her tutor was waiting for her, and was surprised to see a look of confusion on his pale face. She opened the piano and sang a few notes, but Dubrovsky excused himself and broke off the lesson, saying he had a headache; closing the music book, he slipped a note into her hand. Maria Kirilovna, having no time to think, took the note and at once wished she hadn't – but Dubrovsky was no longer there. She went to her room, unfolded the note and read:

> *Come at seven o'clock to the arbour beside the stream. It is essential that I speak to you.*

This greatly excited her curiosity. She had long been expecting him to confess his feelings, wanting and fearing this at the same time. It would be pleasing to hear a confirmation of what she imagined, but she felt it would be improper for her to listen to a confession of love from a man who could never, because of his station in life, hope to win her hand. She decided to keep the tryst, but she was still uncertain about one thing: how to receive this declaration. Should she respond with aristocratic indignation, friendly remonstrances, light-hearted banter or wordless sympathy? In the meantime she kept looking every minute at the clock. It grew dark; candles were lit; Kirila Petrovich sat down to a game of Boston with neighbours who had driven over. The dining-room clock struck a quarter to seven, and Maria Kirilovna quietly went out onto the porch, looked in every direction, and ran into the garden.

The night was dark, the sky was covered with clouds, and it was impossible to make anything out even two yards away, but Maria Kirilovna walked through the dark, along paths she knew, and was close to the arbour in less than a minute. She stopped, wanting to catch her breath, so that she could meet Desforges with an air of unhurried indifference. But there he was, standing before her.

'Thank you,' he said in a quiet, sad voice, 'for not denying my request. I should have been in despair if you hadn't come.'

Maria Kirilovna replied with a sentence she had prepared in advance: 'I hope you will not give me cause to regret my forbearance.'

He said nothing; he seemed to be plucking up his courage.

'Circumstances require… I must leave you,' he said finally. 'Soon, perhaps, you will hear… But I owe you an explanation before we part.'

Maria Kirilovna did not reply. She heard these words as a preface to the confession she was expecting.

'I am not what you think,' he went on, bowing his head. 'I am not the Frenchman Desforges, I am Dubrovsky.'

Maria Kirilovna shrieked.

'Don't be frightened, for the love of God. You mustn't be afraid of my name. Yes, I am the unfortunate man whom your father has deprived of his last crust of bread; I have been driven out of my family home to become a highway robber. But neither on your account nor on his account do you have anything to fear from me. It is all over. I have pardoned him. And it is you – I must tell you – who saved him. My first bloody deed was to have been directed against your father. I was walking up and down beside his house, deciding where the fire should break out, which way to enter his bedroom, how to cut off his ways of escape – and then you passed by, like a heavenly vision, and my heart was overcome. I understood that the house where you live is sacred and that no one related to you by ties of blood can ever be accursed to me. I renounced vengeance as madness. For days on end I wandered about near the gardens of Pokrovskoye, hoping to glimpse your white dress in the distance. I followed you in your carefree walks; I stole from bush to bush, happy in the thought that I was guarding you, that no danger could threaten you where I was secretly present. At last an opportunity arose. I came to live in your house. These three weeks have been a time of happiness for me. The memory of it will be the joy of my sad life. Today I have received news which makes it impossible for me to stay here longer. I am parting from you today… now… But first I had to speak openly to you, so you won't curse me or despise me. Think now and again of Dubrovsky. Be assured that he was born for another destiny, that his soul knew how to love you, that never…'

Just then there was a quiet whistle, and Dubrovsky fell silent. He seized her hand and pressed it to his burning lips. The whistle was repeated.

'Farewell,' said Dubrovsky. 'They're calling me. A minute's delay could be my downfall.' He walked away; Maria Kirilovna remained motionless. Dubrovsky came back and took her hand again.

'If ever,' he said in a tender, touching voice, 'if ever misfortune befalls you and you have no one to help or protect you, will you promise to turn to me – so I can do everything in my power to save you? Will you promise not to scorn my devotion?'

Maria Kirilovna wept silently. There was a third whistle.

'You will be my downfall!' cried Dubrovsky. 'I will not leave you until you give me an answer. Do you promise or not?'

'I promise,' whispered the poor beauty.

Agitated by her tryst with Dubrovsky, Maria Kirilovna began to make her way back to the house. The servants all seemed to be running about; the house was in commotion; there were a lot of people in the yard; a troika stood by the porch. She heard Kirila Petrovich's voice from some way away and hurried inside, fearful lest her absence be noticed. Kirila Petrovich went up to her in the main hall. His guests were standing round the police captain – our old acquaintance – and showering him with questions. Dressed for the road and armed from head to toe, the police captain was answering with a mysterious and preoccupied air.

'Where've you been, Masha?' asked Kirila Petrovich. 'You haven't seen Monsieur Desforges, have you?' Only with difficulty did Masha manage to say no.

'Would you believe it?' Kirila Petrovich went on. 'The police captain's come to arrest him. He insists that Desforges is really Dubrovsky.'

'The distinguishing features tally exactly, Your Excellency,' said the police captain respectfully.

'Hm, dear brother!' said Kirila Petrovich. 'I'll tell you where to go with your distinguishing features. You're not having my Frenchman until I've looked into the matter myself. How can you believe a lying coward like Anton Pafnutich? He must have just dreamt that the tutor wanted to rob him. Why didn't he say anything about it to me at the time?'

58

'The Frenchman gave him quite a fright, Your Excellency. He made him swear to keep silent.'

'It's a pack of lies,' said Kirila Petrovich. 'I'll clear the whole thing up in a moment… Where's the tutor?' he asked a servant who had just come in.

'He can't be found anywhere, sir.'

'Find him then!' shouted Troekurov, beginning to feel uncertain. 'Let me have a look at these distinguishing features of yours,' he went on. The police captain handed him a piece of paper. 'Hm, hm, twenty-three years of age. Maybe – but that doesn't prove very much by itself. Where's the tutor?'

'He can't be found anywhere,' was the answer once more. Kirila Petrovich was now feeling anxious. And Maria Kirilovna was neither alive nor dead.

'You're pale, Masha,' said her father. 'Are you frightened?'

'No, Papa,' she replied. 'I just have a headache.'

'Go off to your room, Masha, and don't be anxious.' Masha kissed his hand and hurried off to her room; there she threw herself on the bed and burst into hysterical sobs. The maidservants ran in, undressed her and, with the help of cold water and every possible kind of smelling salt, managed to calm her down and put her to bed; she fell asleep.

The Frenchman had still not been found. Kirila Petrovich paced up and down the room, ominously whistling, 'Thunder of Victory, Resound!' The guests whispered among themselves; the police captain was beginning to look foolish; the Frenchman was not to be found. He must have had time to escape; he must have been warned. But how, and by whom? That remained a mystery.

The clock struck eleven, but no one was thinking of sleep. In the end Kirila Petrovich said crossly to the police captain, 'Well then? You're not going to stay here till daylight, are you? My house isn't a tavern. You'll have to be smarter than that, brother, to catch Dubrovsky – if that's who it was. Go back home and see if you can move a bit quicker next time… And you can all go home too,' he went on, turning to his guests. 'Order your carriages, I want to go to bed.'

In this ungracious manner Troekurov saw off his guests.

13

Time went by with no incident worthy of note. At the beginning of the following summer, however, life at Pokrovskoye changed in a number of ways.

About twenty miles from Pokrovskoye lay a fine estate called Arbatovo. Prince Vereisky, the owner, had lived for a long time in foreign lands; his estate had been managed by a retired major, and there had been no commerce between it and Pokrovskoye. But at the end of May the Prince returned from abroad and came to live on his estate, which he had never before set eyes on. Accustomed as he was to the dissipations of society, he could not endure solitude, and so, three days after his arrival, he went over to dine with Troekurov, with whom he had at one time been acquainted.

The Prince was about fifty years of age, but he looked much older. Excesses of all kinds had undermined his health and stamped him with their indelible mark. His outward appearance, however, was attractive, even distinguished, and a life spent in society had endowed him with a certain charm, especially in his dealings with women. He had a perpetual need for distraction, and he was perpetually bored. Kirila Petrovich was extremely gratified by his visit, looking on it as a mark of respect from a man who knew the world; in accordance with his usual habit, he treated the Prince to a tour of his estate, including the kennels. But the Prince almost choked in the canine atmosphere and rushed out, pressing a scented handkerchief to his nose. The old-fashioned garden with its clipped limes, rectangular pond and formal paths was not to his taste; he loved English gardens and so-called nature, but he complimented Troekurov and professed to be delighted; then a servant came and announced that dinner was served. They went in. The Prince was limping, exhausted by the walk and wishing he hadn't come to Pokrovskoye.

But they were met in the dining-hall by Maria Kirilovna, and the old philanderer was struck by her beauty. Troekurov seated his guest beside her. Animated by her presence, the Prince was good company, and he managed to capture her attention several times with his interesting stories. After dinner Kirila Petrovich suggested they go out for a ride, but the Prince excused himself, pointing to his velvet boots and joking about his gout; he would prefer to go for a drive, so as not to be separated from his charming companion. A carriage was prepared. The two old men and the young beauty got in and drove off. The conversation never flagged. Maria Kirilovna was enjoying the merry and flattering compliments of a man of the world when Vereisky suddenly turned to Kirila Petrovich and asked about a burned-down building: did it belong to him? Kirila Petrovich frowned; the memories awoken in him by this burned-down estate were unpleasant. He replied that the land was now his, but that it had once belonged to Dubrovsky.

'To Dubrovsky?' Vereisky repeated. 'The famous brigand?'

'To his father,' Troekurov replied, 'who was something of a brigand himself.'

'And what's become of our Rinaldo[18]? Is he still alive? Has he been captured yet?'

'He's alive and at large. And as long as our police captains make common cause with our robbers, he isn't going to be captured. By the way, Prince, didn't he pay a visit to your Arbatovo?'

'Yes, I think he did some burning or plundering last year. But don't you think, Maria Kirilovna, it would be entertaining to make a closer acquaintance with this romantic hero?'

'Pah!' said Troekurov. 'She's acquainted with him already: he gave her music lessons for three whole weeks and he didn't, thank God, exact any payment.' And Kirila Petrovich began to tell the story of his Frenchman. Maria Kirilovna was sitting on thorns. Vereisky listened with deep interest, found it all very strange, and changed the subject. On their return to the house, he ordered his carriage; in spite of Kirila Petrovich's repeated entreaties to stay the night, he left immediately after tea. Before this, however, he invited Kirila Petrovich and Maria Kirilovna to pay him a visit, and the haughty Troekurov accepted; taking into account his princely title, his two stars and the three thousand serfs of his ancestral estate, he looked on Prince Vereisky as to some degree his equal.

Two days after this visit, Kirila Petrovich set off with his daughter to call on Prince Vereisky. As they approached Arbatovo, he couldn't but admire the clean and cheerful-looking huts of the peasants and the stone manor-house built in the style of an English castle. In front of the house stretched a lush green meadow on which Swiss cows were grazing, tinkling their little bells. An extensive park surrounded the house on all sides. The host met his visitors on the porch and gave his arm to the young beauty. They entered a magnificent dining-hall, where the table was set for three. The Prince led his guests to a window, from which there was a charming view. Not far away lay the Volga; loaded barges floated past under full sail; now and again could be seen the small fishing boats so expressively known as death-smacks. Beyond the river were hills and fields, with a few villages animating the landscape. The three of them went on to inspect the gallery of paintings which the Prince had purchased while he was in foreign parts. The Prince explained the subject of each picture to Maria Kirilovna, told her about the painters, and pointed out the merits and shortcomings of their work. He spoke about the paintings with feeling and imagination, not in the conventional language of a pedant. Maria Kirilovna listened to him with pleasure. They went to dine. Troekurov did full justice both to the wines of his Amphitryon[19] and to the artistry of the chef, and Maria Kirilovna felt not a trace of shyness or constraint as she talked to a man she was seeing for only the second time in her life. After dinner the host invited his guests into the garden. They drank coffee on the shore of a broad lake dotted with islands. A brass band struck up; a six-oared boat appeared, then moored just beside the arbour. They went out onto the lake, rowing past the islands and stopping at some of them; on one they found a marble statue, on another a secluded cave, on a third a monument with a mysterious inscription; the young girl's curiosity was piqued by this – and not altogether satisfied by the Prince's courteous reticence; imperceptibly, time passed; it began to grow dark. The Prince hurried his guests back, pleading the evening chill and the dew. He asked Maria Kirilovna to play the role of hostess in the home of an old bachelor. She poured out the tea, listening to the inexhaustible stories of the amiable raconteur; suddenly they heard a bang, and the sky was illuminated by a rocket. The Prince handed Maria Kirilovna a shawl and led her and Troekurov out onto the balcony. Lights of many colours flared up in the darkness, spun round, rose up like sheaves of grain, like palm trees or fountains, fell like showers of rain or stars, faded and flared up again. Maria Kirilovna was as happy as a child. Prince Vereisky was delighted by her pleasure, and Troekurov was much gratified: he took *tous ces frais*[20] as a sign of the Prince's respect, of his desire to please him.

Their supper was in no way less excellent than their dinner. The guests retired to the rooms that had been prepared for them, and in the morning they took leave of their amiable host, all promising to meet again before long.

14

Maria Kirilovna was in her room, sitting by an open window at her embroidery frame. She did not confuse her silks like Konrad's mistress, who, in her amorous distraction, embroidered a rose with green petals.[21] Beneath Maria Kirilovna's needle, the canvas faultlessly repeated the patterns of the original; her thoughts, however, were not on her work – they were far away.

Suddenly a hand was thrust silently through the window; someone placed a letter on the embroidery frame and was gone before Maria Kirilovna could recover from her surprise. Just then a servant entered and called her to Kirila Petrovich. Trembling, she hid the letter under her kerchief and hurried to her father's study.

Kirila Petrovich was not alone. Prince Vereisky was sitting with him. When Maria Kirilovna appeared, the Prince stood up and bowed to her in silence, with an awkwardness that was uncharacteristic of him.

'Come here, Masha,' said Kirila Petrovich. 'I have some news which, I hope, will make you happy. Here is a suitor for you; the Prince is asking for your hand.'

Masha was dumbfounded; her face turned deathly pale. She said nothing. The Prince went up to her, took her hand and asked, visibly moved, if she would consent to make him happy.

'Consent, yes, of course she consents,' said Kirila Petrovich. 'But you know, Prince, how difficult it is for a girl to pronounce that word. Well, children, kiss one another and be happy.'

Masha stood motionless; the old Prince kissed her hand; tears ran down her pale face. The Prince frowned slightly.

'Off with you now, off with you,' said Kirila Petrovich. 'Dry your tears and come back bright and happy… They all weep when they are betrothed,' he went on, turning to Vereisky, 'it's a custom of theirs. And now, Prince, let us talk business – that is, about the dowry.'

Maria Kirilovna eagerly took advantage of this permission to withdraw. She ran to her room, locked herself in and let her tears flow freely, imagining herself as the wife of the old Prince; he had become repulsive and hateful to her. Marriage was as frightening as the executioner's block, as the grave. 'No, no,' she repeated in despair, 'I'd rather die, I'd rather go to a convent, I'd rather marry Dubrovsky.' At this point she remembered the letter and avidly began to read it, sensing it must be from him. It was indeed in Dubrovsky's hand, and it contained only these words:

This evening, ten o'clock, the same place.

15

The moon was shining; it was a quiet July night; now and then a breeze got up and a gentle rustle passed through the garden.

Like a light shadow, the young beauty drew near the meeting-place. There was no one to be seen. Suddenly, from behind the arbour, Dubrovsky appeared before her.

'I know everything,' he said in a quiet, sad voice. 'Remember your promise.'

'You are offering me your protection,' said Masha. 'But – please don't be angry – your protection frightens me. How can you help me?'

'I could rid you of a hateful man.'

'For the love of God, don't touch him. Don't dare to touch him if you love me. I don't want to be the cause of some horror.'

'I won't touch him; your wish is sacred to me. He owes his life to you. No evil deed will ever be committed in your name. You must remain pure even though I commit crimes. But how can I save you from a cruel father?'

'There is still hope. I hope to move him with my tears and my despair. He is obstinate, but he loves me very much.'

'Don't put your trust in empty hopes. In your tears he will see only the usual timidity and revulsion common to all young women who are marrying not for love but out of prudent calculation. What if he takes it into his head to make you happy in spite of yourself? What if you are led to the altar by force, handed over for ever to the power of an aged husband?'

'Then, then we have no choice. Come for me – I shall be your wife.'

Dubrovsky trembled; his pale face flushed crimson, then at once turned paler than before. He remained silent for a long time, his head bowed.

'Gather all the strength of your soul, implore your father, throw yourself at his feet, picture to him all the horror of the future, your youth fading away beside a decrepit and debauched old man, and do not shrink from speaking a cruel truth: say that, if he remains implacable, you will find a terrible protection. Say that wealth will not bring you even one moment of happiness; luxury comforts only the poor – and only for a brief moment before they grow accustomed to it. Don't give up, don't be afraid of his anger or his threats as long as there remains even a shadow of hope. For the love of God, don't give up. But if there's really no other way…'

Dubrovsky buried his face in his hands; he seemed to be choking. Masha was weeping.

'What a wretched, wretched fate,' he said with a bitter sigh. 'I was ready to give my life for you; touching your hand, even seeing you in the distance, was ecstasy for me. And now, when there is an opportunity to clasp you to my agitated heart and say, "Angel, let us die together!", I must beware of bliss, unhappy man that I am, I must thrust it away with all my strength. I dare not fall at your feet and thank Heaven for an inexplicable and undeserved reward. Oh, how I should hate the man who… but I can feel that my heart has no room now for hatred.'

He gently put his arm round her slim waist and gently drew her to his heart. She leant her head trustingly on the shoulder of the young brigand. They were both silent.

65

Time flew. 'I must go,' said Masha at last. Dubrovsky seemed to wake from a trance. He took her hand and placed a ring on her finger.

'If you resolve to turn to me,' he said, 'bring the ring here and drop it into the hollow of this oak. I shall know what to do.'

He kissed her hand and disappeared among the trees.

16

Prince Vereisky's proposal was no longer a secret in the neighbourhood. People offered their congratulations to Kirila Petrovich, and preparations began for the wedding. Day after day Masha put off making any decisive statement. In the meantime, her manner towards her elderly suitor was cold and constrained. The Prince was not troubled by this. He did not require love, being satisfied with her silent consent.

But time was passing. Masha finally resolved to act, and she wrote a letter to Prince Vereisky; she tried to awaken a sense of magnanimity in his heart, openly confessing that she felt not the slightest affection towards him and begging him to renounce his suit and so protect her from her father's power. She quietly slipped the letter into Prince Vereisky's hand; he read it when he was alone, and he was not in the least moved by the frank words of his betrothed. On the contrary, he thought it best to bring forward the date of the wedding; with that in mind, he showed the letter to his future father-in-law.

Kirila Petrovich was enraged; only with difficulty did the Prince persuade him not to reveal to Masha that he had seen her letter. Kirila Petrovich agreed not to speak about it to her, but he, too, considered it best not to waste time and to hold the wedding the very next day. The Prince thought this extremely sensible; he went to his betrothed and told her that her letter had greatly saddened him but that he hoped to win her affection with time: the thought of losing her was more than he could bear, and he did not have the strength to agree to his own death sentence. After that he respectfully kissed her hand and left, saying not a word about Kirila Petrovich's decision.

But his carriage had barely left before her father went into her room and commanded her point-blank to be ready the next day. Maria

Kirilovna, already upset by what Prince Vereisky had said, burst into tears and threw herself at her father's feet.

'Dearest Papa!' she cried pitifully. 'Don't destroy me, Papa! I don't love the Prince, I don't want to be his wife.'

'What do you mean?' Kirila Petrovich asked harshly. 'All this time you have remained silent and been quite agreeable – but now, with everything decided, you turn all capricious and say you've changed your mind. Don't play the fool with me; it'll get you nowhere.'

'Don't destroy me,' poor Masha repeated. 'Why are you driving me away, giving me to a man I don't love? Are you tired of me? I want to be together with you – the same as always. Sweetest Papa, you'll be sad without me, and still sadder when you remember that I'm unhappy. Don't force me, Papenka, I don't want to be married.'

Kirila Petrovich was moved, but he hid his confusion. Pushing her away, he said sternly, 'Nonsense, nonsense! I know better than you what you need for your happiness. Your tears are no use; your wedding day will be the day after tomorrow.'

'The day after tomorrow!' cried Masha. 'Dear God! No, no, that's impossible, it can't be. Papenka, listen, if you have made up your mind to destroy me, then I will find a protector, one you would never imagine – and you will see, you will be appalled to see, what you have driven me to.'

'What? What?' said Troekurov. 'Threats! Are you threatening me, you impudent wench? Well then, you may find me treating you in a way you find hard to imagine. Then we'll learn the name of this protector of yours.'

'Vladimir Dubrovsky,' Masha replied in despair.

Kirila Petrovich thought she had gone mad; he gazed at her, amazed.

'Very well,' he said to her after a silence. 'You can wait for whomever you like to deliver you, but you shall wait here in this room. You won't leave it till the hour of your wedding.' With these words Kirila Petrovich left the room, locking the door behind him.

The poor girl wept for a long time, imagining all that awaited her, but the stormy scene had relieved her soul and she was able to think more calmly about her situation and the best course of action. The important thing was to escape from a hateful marriage; the life of a brigand's wife seemed paradise in comparison with the fate that had been decided for her. She looked at the ring Dubrovsky had left her. She longed fervently to see him alone and talk everything over once more before the decisive moment. That evening, she sensed, she would find Dubrovsky in the garden, beside the arbour; she resolved to go and wait for him there as soon as it grew dark. It grew dark. Masha got ready, but her door had been locked. There was a maid outside; she said she had been forbidden to let her out. Masha was under arrest. Deeply humiliated, she sat by the window and stayed there deep into the night without undressing, her eyes fixed on the dark sky. At dawn she dozed off, but her light sleep was disturbed by sad visions, and the rays of the rising sun soon woke her.

17

She awoke, and the full horror of her position became clear to her with her first thoughts. She rang the bell; a maid came in; in reply to her mistress' questions, she said that Kirila Petrovich had gone to Arbatovo in the evening and had come back late; he had given strict instructions that his daughter be kept in her room and not allowed to speak to anyone; otherwise, there was no sign of any particular preparation for the wedding except that the priest had been ordered under no circumstances to leave the village. After telling her this, the maid left Maria Kirilovna and locked the door again.

These words incensed the young prisoner. Her mind seething, her blood boiling, she resolved to let Dubrovsky know everything, and she began to search for a way of delivering the ring to the hollow of the secret oak. Just then a pebble struck her window, clinking against the pane; Maria Kirilovna looked out into the courtyard and saw little Sasha silently trying to attract her attention. Knowing his devotion to her, she was glad to see him. She opened the window.

'Hello, Sasha,' she said. 'Why are you calling me?'

'I came, sister, to ask if there's anything you need. Papenka is angry, and everyone in the household has been forbidden to take orders from you, but you can ask me anything you like. I'll do what you say.'

'Thank you, dear Sashenka. Do you know the old oak tree by the arbour, the one with a hollow?'

'Yes, sister.'

'Well then, if you love me, run there as quick as you can and put this ring in the hollow. But don't let anyone see you!'

With these words she threw him the ring and closed the window.

The boy picked up the ring, ran off as fast as his legs would carry him, and was beside the secret oak within three minutes. He stopped, gasping for breath, looked all round, and placed the little ring in the hollow. Having successfully accomplished his task, he was about to go and report back to Masha when a raggedy little boy, red-haired and cross-eyed, darted out from behind the arbour, rushed towards the oak and put his hand in the hollow. Quicker than a squirrel, Sasha flew at him and seized him with both hands.

'What are you doing here?' he asked fiercely.

'What's it got to do with you?' asked the boy, trying to free himself.

'Leave that ring alone, carrot-top,' Sasha shouted. 'Or you're in trouble…'

By way of an answer, the boy punched him in the face, but Sasha held on, shouting at the top of his voice, 'Thieves! Thieves! Help! Help!'

The boy struggled to get away. He looked a couple of years older than Sasha, and he was much stronger; but Sasha was the more agile. They fought for several minutes, until the red-headed boy finally got the upper hand. He threw Sasha to the ground and seized him round the throat.

But just then a powerful hand grabbed him by his red, bristly hair, and Stepan the gardener lifted Sasha a good foot clear of the ground.

'Ginger brute!' said the gardener. 'How dare you hit the young master?'

Sasha quickly leapt to his feet and got his breath back.

'You had me under the armpits,' he said. 'Otherwise you'd never have been able to throw me. Give me the ring now and clear off.'

'Not likely,' said the red-headed boy, suddenly spinning round and freeing his bristles from Stepan's grip. He sped off but Sasha caught up with him and shoved him in the back, and the boy fell headlong. The gardener seized him a second time and secured him with his belt.

'Give me the ring!' Sasha shouted.

'Wait a moment, young master,' said Stepan. 'We'll take him to the steward – he'll know what to do with him.'

The gardener led the prisoner to the main courtyard, and Sasha went with them, looking anxiously now and again at his trousers, which were torn and grass-stained. Suddenly all three found themselves face to face with Kirila Petrovich, who was on his way to inspect the stables.

'What's going on?' he asked Stepan.

Stepan briefly described all that had happened. Kirila Petrovich listened attentively.

'Little rascal,' he said, turning to Sasha, 'what were you fighting about?'

'He stole the ring from the hollow oak, Papenka. Tell him to give me back the ring!'

'What ring? What hollow oak?'

'The one Maria Kirilovna… The ring…'

Sasha stammered in confusion. Kirila Petrovich frowned and said, shaking his head, 'So Maria Kirilovna's mixed up in all this, is she? You'd better make a clean breast of it now – or I'll thrash you within an inch of your life.'

'I swear, Papenka, I, Papenka… Maria Kirilovna didn't ask me to do anything, Papenka.'

'Stepan, go and cut me a birch switch, a nice young one.'

'Wait, Papenka, I'll tell you everything. I was running about in the yard, and my sister opened the window, and I ran there, and Maria Kirilovna threw down the ring accidentally, and I hid it in the hollow oak, and… and… this red-headed boy tried to steal the ring…'

'Threw down the ring accidentally – and you tried to hide it… Stepan, get me some switches.'

'Wait, Papenka, let me tell you everything. My sister Maria Kirilovna told me to run down to the oak and put the ring in the hollow, but this horrid boy…'

Kirila Petrovich turned to the horrid boy and asked sternly, 'Where are you from?'

'I am a house serf of the Dubrovsky family,' answered the red-headed boy.

Kirila Petrovich's face darkened.

'It seems you don't acknowledge me as your master – very well. And what were you doing in my garden?'

'Stealing raspberries,' the boy answered, with great equanimity.

'Ah, I see! like master, like man; judge the flock by its priest. And do raspberries really grow on my oak trees?'

The boy said nothing.

'Papenka, tell him to give me back the ring,' said Sasha.

'Quiet, Sasha,' said Kirila Petrovich, 'And remember – I haven't finished with you yet. Go to your room. And you, squint-eyes, you seem like a bright lad. Give back the ring and be off with you.'

The boy opened his fist and showed there was nothing in it.

'If you tell me everything, I won't thrash you. I'll even give you five kopeks so you can buy yourself some nuts. But if you don't, you'll find you get more than you've bargained for. Well?'

The boy said nothing. He hung his head and looked as if he were a half-wit.

'Very well,' said Kirila Petrovich, 'Lock him up somewhere and make sure he doesn't get out – or I'll skin the lot of you.'

Stepan took the boy to the dovecote, locked him up there, and told Agafya, the old poultry woman, to keep watch on him.

'We must send for the police captain,' said Kirila Petrovich, following the boy with his eyes, 'and as quickly as possible.'

'There's no doubt about it. She's kept up with that accursed Dubrovsky. But has she really been appealing to him for help?' thought Kirila Petrovich, pacing about the room and angrily whistling 'Thunder of Victory, Resound!' 'Maybe, after all this time, I'm hot on his heels! Yes, he won't slip away from us now. We must seize the opportunity. Ha! A bell! The Lord be praised – it's the police captain… Hey, fetch that little brat we've just captured.'

A cart had driven into the yard. Our old acquaintance the police captain, covered in dust, entered the room.

'Splendid news,' said Kirila Petrovich. 'I've caught Dubrovsky.'

'The Lord be praised, Your Excellency!' said the delighted police captain. 'Where is he?'

'That is, not Dubrovsky himself, but one of his gang. They're bringing him in. He'll help us to capture the chieftain. Here he is.'

The police captain, expecting a fearsome brigand, was amazed to see a rather puny-looking thirteen-year-old boy. He turned to Kirila Petrovich in bewilderment, waiting for an explanation. Kirila Petrovich then related the events of the morning, without, however, mentioning Maria Kirilovna.

The police captain listened attentively, glancing frequently at the boy; the little rascal was pretending to be an idiot and seemed to be paying no attention at all to anything going on around him.

'Allow me, Your Excellency, to have a word with you in private,' said the police captain finally.

Kirila Petrovich took him to another room and locked the door.

Half an hour later they returned to the hall, where the prisoner was waiting for his fate to be decided.

'The master wanted to have you locked up in the town gaol, given a good thrashing and sent to Siberia,' said the police captain, 'but I interceded on your behalf and won you a pardon... Untie him!'

The boy was untied.

'Thank your master,' said the police captain. The boy went up to Kirila Petrovich and kissed his hand.

'You go home now,' said Kirila Petrovich, 'and don't go stealing any more raspberries from hollow oaks.'

The boy went out, jumped joyfully down the front steps and, without looking back, dashed off across the fields to Kistenevka. When he got there, he stopped at a little tumbledown hut, at the very edge of the village, and knocked at the window; the window opened, and an old woman looked out.

'Give me some bread, Granny,' said the boy. 'I've had nothing to eat since breakfast, I'm starving.'

'Ah, it's you, Mitya. But where've you been all day, you little devil?' said the old woman.

'I'll tell you later, Granny. For the love of God, give me some bread!'

'Come inside then.'

'I haven't got time, Granny. I have to go somewhere, I'm in a hurry. Bread – give me some bread, for the love of Christ!'

'All right, you little madcap, here you are!' the old woman muttered, and thrust a piece of black bread through the window. The boy greedily bit into it and rushed off, still chewing.

It was beginning to grow dark. Mitya made his way past barns and vegetable plots to the Kistenevka wood. When he came to two pine trees standing like sentinels at the edge of the wood, he stopped, looked carefully all round, let out a shrill staccato whistle, then stood and listened; there was a long soft answering whistle and someone came out of the wood towards him.

18

Kirila Petrovich was walking up and down the hall, whistling his tune more loudly than ever; the entire house was in commotion, servants were running backwards and forwards, maids were bustling about, coachmen were preparing the carriage, and the yard was crowded with people. Maria Kirilovna was in her dressing-room; a lady surrounded by servants was standing in front of a mirror and attending to her. The young mistress was pale and motionless; her head was drooping languidly under the weight of her diamonds; sometimes she gave a slight start when she was pricked by a careless hand, but she said nothing, gazing vacantly into the mirror.

'Are you nearly ready?' called Kirila Petrovich.

'In a moment,' replied the lady. 'Maria Kirilovna, stand up and look at yourself. Is everything in order?'

Maria Kirilovna got to her feet and said nothing. The door opened.

'The bride is ready,' the lady said to Kirila Petrovich. 'You can tell her to take her place in the carriage.'

'With God's blessing,' Kirila Petrovich replied, taking an icon from the table. 'Come here, Masha,' he said to her with emotion, 'let me give you my blessing.' The poor girl fell at his feet and burst out sobbing.

'Papenka, Papenka…' she said through her tears, and her voice failed her. Kirila Petrovich hurriedly blessed her. She was helped to her feet and almost carried out to the carriage. The matron of honour[22] and a maidservant got in with her. They drove to the church. The bridegroom was already waiting for them. He came out to greet the bride and was struck by her pallor and her strange look. Together they entered the cold, empty church; the doors were locked behind them. The priest came out from behind the iconostasis and immediately began. Maria Kirilovna saw nothing, heard nothing and could think of only one thing; she had been waiting for Dubrovsky since early that morning, not for one moment had hope left her, but when the priest turned to her with the customary questions, she shuddered and felt faint yet remained silent, still waiting. The priest, receiving no answer from her, pronounced the irrevocable words.

The ceremony was over. She felt the cold kiss of a husband she did not love, she heard joyful words of congratulation, and she was still unable to believe that her life had been fettered for ever and that Dubrovsky had not rushed to her rescue. The Prince turned to her with tender words which she did not understand. They left the church; the porch was crowded with peasants from Pokrovskoye. She ran her gaze quickly over them and slipped back into her former apathy. Bride and groom got into the carriage together and set off for Arbatovo; Kirila Petrovich had gone on ahead in order to greet them on their arrival. Alone with his young wife, the Prince was not in the least troubled by her cold manner. He did not irritate her with cloying protestations and absurd raptures; his words were simple and required no reply. So they drove for about seven miles, the horses going at a fast trot over the bumps of the country road and the carriage barely swaying on its English springs. Suddenly they heard shouting, the carriage stopped, a crowd of armed men surrounded it, and a man in a half mask, opening the door beside the young Princess, said to her, 'You are free. Get down.' 'What's all this?' shouted the Prince, 'and who are you?' 'It's Dubrovsky,' said the Princess. The Prince, not losing his presence of mind, took a travelling-pistol from a side-pocket and shot at the masked brigand. The Princess shrieked in horror and covered her face with her hands. Dubrovsky was wounded in the shoulder; he was bleeding. The Prince immediately took out another pistol, but he was given no time to use it; the door on his side opened, and several strong hands dragged him out of the carriage and snatched the pistol away. Knives flashed above him.

'Don't touch him!' shouted Dubrovsky, and his grim comrades drew back.

'You are free,' Dubrovsky repeated, turning to the pale Princess.

'No,' she answered. 'It's too late. I am married, I am the wife of Prince Vereisky.'

'What are you saying?' Dubrovsky cried out in despair. 'No, you are not his wife, you were coerced, you could never have given your consent.'

'I consented, I made a vow,' she replied firmly. 'The Prince is my husband. Tell your men to let him go, and leave me with him. I did not deceive you. I waited for you until the last minute. But now, I tell you, now it is too late. Release us.'

But Dubrovsky could no longer hear her: the pain from his wound and the turbulence in his soul had taken away his strength. He collapsed beside one of the carriage wheels, and his men gathered round him. He managed to say a few words, and they put him on his horse. Two of them supported him, a third led the horse by the bridle, and they went off across the fields, leaving the carriage in the middle of the road, the servants bound and the horses unharnessed; but they had neither stolen anything nor shed a single drop of blood in revenge for the blood of their chief.

19

In a narrow clearing deep in the forest was a small stronghold consisting of a ditch and a rampart, behind which were a few huts and dugouts.

A number of men, immediately identifiable as brigands from their motley dress and the fact that they all bore arms, were eating their dinner in this enclosure, sitting around a communal cauldron. A sentry was sitting on the rampart beside a small cannon, his legs tucked under him; he was sewing a patch onto one of his garments, plying his needle with the skill of an experienced tailor while continually looking about him in every direction.

Although a cup had been passed round several times, a strange silence reigned over the gathering. The brigands finished their dinner and, one after another, got to their feet and said their prayers; some went to their huts while others wandered off into the forest or lay down for a brief nap as Russians do.

The sentry finished his sewing, shook out the tattered garment, admired the patch, stuck the needle into his sleeve, and burst out, at the top of his voice, into an old melancholy song:

'*Green mother, green dubrovka*[23]*, don't rustle,*
Don't stop a young lad from dreaming his dreams.'

The door of one of the huts opened and an old woman in a white cap, dressed neatly and primly, appeared on the threshold. 'Enough of that, Stepka,' she said angrily. 'The master's resting – and you have to start bawling. Are you all without conscience or pity?' 'I beg pardon, Yegorovna,' Stepka answered. 'Don't worry, I'll be quiet now. Let the young master sleep and get his strength back!' The old woman went back into the hut, and Stepka began pacing about the rampart.

Inside the hut, lying on a campbed behind a partition, was the wounded Dubrovsky. His pistols were on a small table beside him, and his sword was hanging at the head of the bed. The floor and walls of the mud hut were covered by rich rugs, and in one corner stood a lady's silvered dressing-table and mirror. Dubrovsky had an open book in his hand, but his eyes were closed. And the old woman, who kept peeping round from the other side of the partition, could not be sure whether he was asleep or merely lost in thought.

Suddenly Dubrovsky started; an alarm sounded inside the stronghold, and Stepka thrust his head through the window. 'Vladimir Andreevich, sir!' he shouted. 'They're on our track! Our men have just signalled.' Dubrovsky leapt out of bed, seized his weapons and went outside. The brigands, who had been milling about noisily, fell silent. 'Are you all here?' asked Dubrovsky. 'All except the scouts,' came the answer. 'To your positions!' Dubrovsky shouted, and each man took up his position. Then three scouts came running towards the gates. Dubrovsky went to meet them. 'What's happening?' he asked. 'There are soldiers in the wood,' they replied. 'We're being surrounded.' Dubrovsky ordered the gate to be locked and went over to check the small cannon. There were voices in the wood; they were coming closer.

The brigands waited in silence. Three or four soldiers appeared out of the forest and at once drew back again, firing shots as a signal to their comrades. 'Prepare for battle!' said Dubrovsky. There was a murmur from among the brigands, then everything went silent. They heard the noise of approaching soldiers; weapons glinted from between the trees, and around a hundred and fifty men poured out of the wood and rushed, shouting, towards the rampart. Dubrovsky lit the fuse; the cannon fired; one soldier had his head torn off and two were wounded. The soldiers were thrown into confusion but their officer dashed forwards and the soldiers followed, rushing into the ditch; the brigands shot at them with guns and pistols and then waited, holding their axes ready: the frenzied soldiers, having left around twenty wounded comrades in the ditch below, were now trying to climb the rampart. There was a hand-to-hand struggle. The soldiers had reached the top of the rampart and the brigands were beginning to lose ground, but Dubrovsky got right up to the officer, put his pistol to his chest and fired; the man fell backwards. A group of soldiers picked him up in their arms and quickly carried him back into the forest; the others, having lost their leader, stopped. Emboldened, the brigands took advantage of this moment of confusion, pressing the soldiers back and forcing them down into the ditch. The soldiers took flight and the brigands chased after them, yelling and shrieking. The battle was won. Confident that the enemy had been routed, Dubrovsky called his men off, gave orders to bring in the wounded and shut himself away in his stronghold, doubling the number of sentries and forbidding anyone to leave.

After this battle the government began to pay more serious attention to Dubrovsky's daring robberies. Intelligence about the places he frequented was gathered. A detachment of soldiers was sent out, ordered to capture him dead or alive. A few members of his band were caught, and it was learnt that Dubrovsky was no longer among them. A few days after the battle he had gathered together his companions, announced that he was leaving them for good, and advised them to change their way of life. 'You have grown rich under my command and each of you has a pass with which you can make your way to some distant province and live there for the rest of your life, working honestly and prosperously. But you're all rascals and you probably won't want to give up your present trade.' After this speech he left them, taking with him only one man. No one knew what had become of him. At first the authorities doubted this testimony: the brigands' devotion to their chief was well known. It was supposed that they were trying to shield him. Subsequent events, however, confirmed that the brigands had spoken the truth: the raids, fires and robberies came to an end. The roads became safe. From other reports it was learnt that Dubrovsky had escaped abroad.

NOTES

1. The dried beetle, *Cantharis vesicatoria* or Spanish fly, was used to stimulate the circulation.

2. Pushkin has just told us that Dubrovsky is in, not the Horse Guards, but the Foot Guards. *Dubrovsky* is unfinished; it contains other minor inconsistencies.

3. She means St Nicholas' Day, 9th May.

4. From 'Ode on the Death of Prince Meshchersky' by Derzhavin (1743–1816).

5. The first line of another poem by Derzhavin, celebrating the capture of Ismail, in 1791, from the Turks. It was set to music by Kozlovsky.

6. A low four-wheeled open carriage.

7. A reference to what was once a common belief in Russia: meeting a priest coming in the opposite direction was thought to bring bad luck.

8. i.e. during the Russo-Turkish war of 1787–91.

9. Johann Lavater, born in Zurich in 1741, wrote a long work on the art of judging character from a person's facial features and general build.

10. Before Peter the Great banned it during his Westernising reforms, the kaftan was a standard item of Russian male dress. The ban was rescinded during the nineteenth century, but the kaftan continued to be seen as provincial or old-fashioned.

11. An important Russian general from the time of the Napoleonic wars.

12. 'What does Monsieur want?'

13. Schoolboy French for 'I want to sleep in your room'.

14. 'Gladly, Monsieur. Please make the necessary arrangements.'

15. More schoolboy French, for 'I want to talk to you'.

16. 'What is it, Monsieur, what is it?'

17. 'Upon my word, officer'.

18. The hero of Christiane Vulpius' *Rinaldo Rinaldini* (1798), a Robin Hood figure.

19. In Greek mythology, the husband of Alcmene and step-father of Heracles; Zeus took on his form to give a vast feast, giving rise to the proverbial use of the name Amphitryon to signify any rich and generous host.

20. All this expense.

21. A reference to 'Konrad Valenrod' (1828) by the great Polish poet, and friend of Pushkin, Adam Mickiewicz (1798–1855). Musing on the absence of her beloved Konrad, the heroine embroiders a rose in green, and its leaves in red.

22. Or more precisely: the family friend who, in accordance with Russian custom, is substituting for Maria Kirilovna's long-dead mother.

23. Oak-grove. The hero's surname is derived from this word.

Egyptian Nights

1

– Quel est cet homme?
– Ha! C'est un bien grand talent, il fait de sa voix tout ce qu'il veut.
– Il devrait bien, madame, s'en faire une culotte.[1]

Charsky was a native citizen of St Petersburg. He was not yet thirty; he was unmarried; his work in the civil service was not burdensome. His late uncle, a vice-governor during prosperous times, had left him a decent estate. His life could have been most pleasant; but he had the misfortune to write and publish poetry. In journals he was called a poet; in servants' quarters a scribbler.

In spite of the great advantages enjoyed by bards – it has to be said: apart from the right to use the accusative case instead of the genitive and a few other examples of so-called poetic licence, we know of no particular advantages enjoyed by Russian bards – be that as it may, in spite of all their possible advantages, these people are also subject to great disadvantages and unpleasantnesses. The bard's bitterest, most unbearable affliction is his title, his sobriquet, with which he is branded and from which he can never escape. The public look on him as their property; in their opinion, he is born for their benefit and pleasure. Should he return from the country, the first person he meets will greet him with: 'Haven't you brought anything new for us?' Should he be deep in thought about the disorder of his affairs, or about the illness of someone close to him, a trite smile will at once accompany the trite exclamation: 'No doubt you're composing something?' Should he fall in love, his beautiful one will buy herself an album from the English Shop and be waiting for elegies. If he goes to visit someone he hardly knows, to talk about an important matter, the man will summon his son and make him read *this gentleman's* poems aloud – and the little boy will treat the bard to the bard's own, mangled, poems. And if these are the laurels of the craft, then imagine its pains! The greetings, requests, albums and little boys were so irritating, Charsky confessed, that he had to be constantly on his guard lest he let slip some offensive remark.

83

Charsky made every possible effort to escape the insufferable sobriquet. He avoided his fellow men of letters, preferring the company of even the most vacuous members of high society. His conversation was exceedingly banal and never touched on literature. In his dress he always followed the latest fashion with the diffidence and superstition of a young Muscovite visiting St Petersburg for the very first time. His study, furnished like a lady's bedroom, did not in any respect call to mind that of a writer; no books were piled on or under the tables; the sofa was not stained with ink; there was none of the disorder which reveals the presence of the Muse and the absence of dustpan and brush. Charsky despaired if one of his society friends discovered him pen in hand. It is hard to believe that a man endowed with talent and a soul could stoop to such petty dissimulation. He would pretend to be a passionate lover of horses, a desperate gambler or the most discriminating of gourmets – even though he could not tell a mountain pony from an Arab steed, could never remember trumps and secretly preferred baked potatoes to every possible invention of French cuisine. He led the most distracted of lives; he was there at every ball, he ate too much at every diplomatic dinner, and at every reception he was as inevitable as Rezanov's ice-cream.

But he was a poet, and his passion was not to be overcome: when he sensed the approach of that 'nonsense' (his word for inspiration), Charsky would lock himself in his study and write from morning till late at night. Only then, he would confess to his closest friends, did he know true happiness. The rest of the time he went out and about, put on airs, dissembled and listened again and again to the famous question: 'Haven't you written anything new?'

One morning Charsky was in that state of grace when fancies outline themselves clearly before you and you discover vivid, unexpected words to embody your visions, when verses flow readily from your pen and resonant rhymes come forward to meet orderly thoughts. His soul was deep in sweet forgetfulness – and society, society's opinions and his own foibles no longer existed for him. He was writing poetry.

Suddenly his study door creaked and a head came round it. Charsky started and frowned.

'Who's that?' he asked in annoyance, mentally cursing his servants for always leaving his vestibule unattended.

The stranger entered.

He was tall and lean, and he looked about thirty. The features of his dark face were distinctive: a pale, high forehead shaded by dark locks, gleaming black eyes, an aquiline nose, and a thick beard framing sunken, bronzed cheeks – all these made it clear he was a foreigner. He was wearing a black frock-coat, turning white along the seams, and summer trousers (even though it was now well into autumn), and on his yellowish shirt front, beneath a worn black cravat, shone a false diamond; his fraying hat had clearly seen both sun and rain. Meeting this man in a forest, you'd take him for a brigand; in society – for a political conspirator; in your vestibule – for a charlatan peddling elixirs and arsenic.

'What do you want?' Charsky asked him, in French.

'Signor,' the foreigner answered with low bows, *'Lei voglia perdonarmi se…'*[2]

Charsky did not offer him a chair but stood up himself. The conversation continued in Italian.

'I am a Neapolitan artist,' said the stranger. 'Circumstances have obliged me to leave my homeland. Trusting in my talent, I have come to Russia.'

Charsky thought the Neapolitan intended to give some cello recitals and was selling tickets door to door. He was about to hand the man his twenty-five roubles, to get rid of him quickly, but the stranger went on:

'I hope, Signor, that you will be able to assist a fellow-artist and introduce me to the houses where you yourself are received.'

No blow to Charsky's vanity could have been sharper. He looked haughtily at the man who called himself his fellow-artist.

'Allow me to ask who I am speaking to and who you take me to be,' he said, struggling to hold back his indignation.

The Neapolitan sensed Charsky's annoyance.

'Signore,' he stammered, *'ho creduto… ho sentito… vostra Eccellenza mi perdonerà…'*[3]

'What do you want?' Charsky asked dryly.

'I have heard a great deal about your astonishing talent; I am certain that gentlemen here consider it an honour to offer their patronage in every possible way to so outstanding a poet,' the Italian replied, 'and I have therefore taken the liberty of presenting myself to you…'

'You are mistaken, Signor,' Charsky interrupted. 'The title of poet does not exist here. Our poets do not enjoy the patronage of gentlemen; our poets are themselves gentlemen, and if our Maecenases (the devil take them!) don't know this, then so much the worse for them. Here we have no tattered abbés whom a composer might take off the street to write a libretto. Our poets don't go on foot from door to door, soliciting donations.[4] And whoever told you I am a great bard must have been jesting. I admit I did once write a few poor epigrams, but, thank God, I neither have nor wish to have anything to do with our bards.'

The poor Italian was in confusion. He glanced round the room. The paintings, the marble statues and bronze busts, the expensive gewgaws displayed on Gothic etageres, astonished him. He understood that there was nothing in common between himself, a poor wandering artiste in a worn cravat and an old frock-coat, and this haughty dandy standing before him in a tufted brocade skullcap and a gold-embroidered Chinese gown with a Turkish shawl for a belt. He uttered some incoherent excuses, bowed, and was about to leave. His pathetic look moved Charsky who, for all his affectations, had a kind and noble heart. He felt ashamed of the touchiness of his vanity.

'Where are you going?' he said to the Italian. 'Wait. I had to decline an undeserved title and confess to you that I am no poet. Now let us talk about your affairs. I am ready to be of service to you in any way that I can. You are a musician?'

'No, *Eccellenza*!' the Italian answered. 'I am a poor *improvvisatore*.'

'An *improvvisatore*!' exclaimed Charsky, sensing all the cruelty of his behaviour. 'Why didn't you say at once that you're an *improvvisatore*?' And Charsky pressed the Italian's hand with a sense of genuine remorse.

His friendly air was reassuring. Straightforwardly, the Italian began to deliver himself of his proposal. His outward appearance was not deceptive. He needed money; he was hoping, here in Russia, to get his personal affairs onto a sounder footing. Charsky listened to him attentively.

'I hope,' he said to the poor artist, 'that you will enjoy success; society here has never heard an *improvvisatore* before. Curiosity will be aroused. Italian, I admit, is not spoken here, so you will not be understood; but that doesn't matter; what matters is that you should be in vogue.'

'But if no one here understands Italian,' said the *improvvisatore*, after a little thought, 'who will come and listen to me?'

'They will come, don't worry; some out of curiosity, some for a way of passing the evening, and others to show they understand Italian. All that matters, I repeat, is that you should be in vogue – and you will be in vogue, you have my word for it.'

After noting his address, Charsky parted affectionately with the *improvvisatore*, and that very evening he began making arrangements on his behalf.

2

'I'm Tsar and slave, I'm worm and God.'

The following day Charsky was walking down a dark, dirty tavern corridor in search of Room 35. He stopped at the door and knocked. Yesterday's Italian opened it.

'Victory!' said Charsky. 'Everything's as good as done. The Princess *** is lending you her hall; at a reception last night I managed to recruit half of Petersburg; you must print your tickets and announcements. I guarantee you, if not a triumph, at least some profit.'

'That's what matters most!' exclaimed the Italian, showing his joy through the lively gestures of a man from the South. 'I knew you would help me. *Corpo di Bacco!*[5] You're a poet, just as I am; and say what you like, poets are splendid fellows! How can I express my gratitude? Wait… would you like to hear an improvisation?'

'An improvisation! But surely you need an audience, and music, and the thunder of applause?'

'Nonsense, nonsense! Where can I find a better audience? You are a poet, you will understand me better than anyone, and your quiet

encouragement means more to me than a whole storm of applause...
Find somewhere to sit and give me a theme.'

Charsky sat down on a trunk (one of the two chairs in the cramped little kennel was broken, the other covered by a heap of papers and linen). The *improvvisatore* took a guitar from the table – and stood facing Charsky, plucking the strings with bony fingers and waiting for his command.

'Here's a theme for you,' said Charsky. '*A poet chooses the matter of his songs himself; the crowd has no right to direct his inspiration.*'

The Italian's eyes gleamed; he played a few chords, proudly flung back his head – and impassioned stanzas, the expression of immediate feeling, flew harmoniously from his lips. Here they are, transcribed freely by a friend of ours from the words preserved in Charsky's memory.

> *Here comes the poet – he can see*
> *No one, and yet he's open-eyed.*
> *Then someone's pulling at his sleeve*
> *And he must listen while they chide:*
> *'No sooner have you climbed to heaven*
> *Than back to earth you cast your eyes;*
> *By what strange power are you driven*
> *To wander down such aimless ways?*
> *A fruitless fever grips your soul;*
> *Your vision's blurred, your view's obscured;*
> *It seems you can't escape the hold*
> *Of matters pointless and absurd.*
> *A genius soars above the earthy;*
> *True poets sense an obligation*
> *Only to sing what's truly worthy*
> *The Muses and their inspiration...'*
> *'...What makes a wind sweep down ravines*
> *And whirl dry leaves through dusty air,*
> *While ships becalmed on silent seas*
> *Wait for its kiss in numb despair?*
> *What makes an eagle leave his height*

And, flying past towers, choose to alight
On some old stump? The eagle knows.
And Desdemona's heart is closed
To all but black Othello, whom
She loves just as the moon adores
The blackest night. Hearts know no laws;
Eagles and winds are free to roam.
A poet too is like the wind;
He too escapes all ties that bind.
And like the eagle, he flies far;
Like Desdemona, he must love
Whatever idol charms his heart,
And not care who may disapprove.'

The Italian fell silent. Charsky said nothing, amazed and moved.

'Well?' asked the *improvvisatore*.

Charsky took his hand and pressed it firmly.

'Well?' asked the *improvvisatore*. 'What do you think?'

'Astonishing!' said the poet. 'How can this be? Another person's thought has barely reached your ears – and at once you make it your own, as if you've been nursing it, cherishing it, tirelessly developing it. For you, then, there exists neither labour, nor dejection, nor the anxiety that precedes inspiration. Astonishing, quite astonishing!'

The *improvvisatore* answered, 'Every talent is inexplicable. How is it that a sculptor, seeing a slab of Carrara marble, can glimpse a hidden Jupiter and bring him out into the light, splitting the stone casing with hammer and chisel?[6] Why does a thought leave a poet's head already equipped with four rhymes and divided into feet that are harmonious and of equal length? Similarly, no one but the *improvvisatore* himself can understand this quickness of impressions, this intimate link between his own inspiration and the will of a stranger. Even my own attempts to explain this would be in vain. However… it's time to think about my first evening. What do you suggest? How should tickets be priced so as neither to burden the public nor leave me out of pocket? La Signora Catalani, they say, charged twenty-five roubles. That's not a bad price.'

Charsky found it unpleasant to be brought down so suddenly from the heights of poetry into the bookkeeper's office; but he well understood the imperative of everyday need, and, together with the Italian, he plunged into matters pecuniary. The Italian then revealed such unbridled greed, such an unabashed love of profit, that Charsky felt disgusted by him and hastened to leave, so as not to lose entirely the sense of wonder aroused in him by the brilliant *improvvisatore*. The preoccupied Italian did not notice this change; he accompanied Charsky along the corridor and down the staircase, seeing him off with deep bows and assurances of eternal gratitude.

3

Tickets are ten roubles each;
the performance begins at 7 p.m.

A poster

Princess ***'s reception hall had been placed at the *improvvisatore*'s disposal. A stage had been erected, and chairs had been set out in twelve rows; on the appointed day, at seven o'clock, the hall was lit up and an old long-nosed woman, wearing a grey hat with broken feathers and with rings on all her fingers, sat at a little table by the door, checking and selling tickets. Gendarmes stood by the main entrance. The audience began to gather. Charsky was among the first to arrive. He was very concerned that the performance should be a success, and he wanted to see the *improvvisatore* and find out if he was satisfied with everything. He found the Italian in a little side room, glancing impatiently at his watch. The Italian was dressed theatrically: he was in black from head to toe; the lace collar of his shirt was turned back, the strange whiteness of his bare neck stood out sharply against his thick black beard, and locks of hair hung down over his forehead and eyebrows. Charsky greatly disliked all this, finding it unpleasant to see a poet in the costume of a travelling player. After a brief conversation, he returned to the hall, which was filling up steadily.

Soon the chairs were all occupied by dazzling ladies; tightly framing the ladies, the men stood in front of the stage, along the walls and behind the last row of chairs. The musicians and their music stands took up both sides of the stage. On a table in the middle stood a porcelain vase. There were a lot of people. Everyone was waiting impatiently. At half-past seven the musicians finally bestirred themselves; they raised their bows and began the overture to *Tancredi*[7]. The last notes of the overture thundered out; everything went still and silent. And the *improvvisatore*, greeted by deafening applause from all sides, advanced with low bows to the very edge of the stage.

Charsky had been feeling anxious, wondering what impression the first minute would make, but he noticed that the Italian's costume, which to him had seemed so unfortunate, appeared otherwise to the audience. Charsky himself found nothing absurd in the man when he saw him on stage, his pallid face brightly lit by a multitude of candles and lamps. The applause died away; conversation ceased. The Italian, expressing himself in broken French, asked the ladies and gentlemen present to propose some themes, writing them down on separate bits of paper. At this unanticipated invitation, the audience all began looking at one another in silence; not one of them responded. The Italian waited a little, then repeated his request in a timid and deferential voice. Charsky was standing right by the stage; he was seized with anxiety; he sensed that nothing would happen without him and that he would have to write down a theme himself. Several women's heads had indeed turned towards him and begun to call out his name, at first softly, then louder and louder. Hearing this, the *improvvisatore* looked round for Charsky, saw him there at his feet, and, with a friendly smile, handed him pencil and paper. Charsky found it most unpleasant to have to play a role in this comedy, but he had no choice: he took the pencil and paper from the Italian's hands and wrote a few words; the Italian took the vase from the table, stepped down from the stage, and held the vase out to Charsky, who dropped in his piece of paper. This set an effective example: two journalists considered it their duty as men of letters to write down a theme each; the secretary of the Neapolitan embassy and some young man, only recently returned from his travels and still raving about Florence, placed their folded papers in the urn; lastly, at her mother's bidding, a plain young girl with tears in her eyes wrote a few lines in Italian and, blushing to her ears, handed them to the *improvvisatore*; the ladies watched in silence, with faint smiles of mockery. Returning to his stage, the *improvvisatore* put the urn back on the table and began, one by one, to take out the pieces of paper, reading each out aloud:

The Cenci family (La famiglia dei Cenci).
L'ultimo giorno di Pompei.
Cleopatra e i suoi amanti.
La primavera veduta da una prigione.
Il trionfo di Tasso.[8]

'What is the wish of the esteemed company?' asked the deferential Italian. 'Will you yourselves select one of the proposed themes, or will you let the matter be decided by lot?'

'By lot!' said a voice from the crowd.

'By lot, by lot!' the audience repeated.

The *improvvisatore* stepped down again from the stage, holding the urn in his hands, and asked, 'Who will be so kind as to draw a theme?' The *improvvisatore* looked entreatingly up and down the front rows. Not one of the dazzling ladies moved a finger. The *improvvisatore*, unaccustomed to northern indifference, seemed agitated. Then, over to one side, he noticed a raised hand, in a small white glove; he quickly turned round and walked up to a majestic young beauty sitting at the end of the second row. She stood up without any embarrassment and, with the utmost simplicity, put her small aristocratic hand into the urn and drew out a folded slip of paper.

'Be so kind as to unfold the paper and read it out,' said the *improvvisatore*. The beauty unfolded the paper and read out aloud: '*Cleopatra e i suoi amanti.*'

These words were pronounced quietly but such was the silence reigning over the hall that everyone heard them. The *improvvisatore* bowed, with an air of deep gratitude, to the beautiful lady and returned to his stage.

'Ladies and gentlemen,' he said, turning to the audience, 'The lot proposes I improvise on the theme of Cleopatra and her lovers.

I humbly ask whoever chose this theme to clarify their thought: which lovers did they have in mind, *perché la grande regina n'aveva molti?*[9]

At these words many of the men burst into loud laughter. The *improvvisatore* appeared somewhat confused.

'I should like to know,' he went on, 'what historical moment was in the mind of the person who proposed this theme... I shall be most grateful if they can clarify this.'

No one hurried to answer. Several ladies glanced at the plain young girl who had written down a theme at her mother's bidding. The poor girl noticed this unkind attention and was in such confusion that tears appeared on her eyelashes. Charsky could not bear this and, turning to the *improvvisatore*, he said to him in Italian, 'It was I who suggested the theme. I had in mind the testimony of Victor Aurelius, who maintains that Cleopatra proposed death as the price of her love and that there were admirers neither frightened nor repelled by this condition. I think, however, that the subject is a little difficult. Perhaps you would prefer to choose another?'

But the *improvvisatore* could already sense the approach of the god. He signalled to the musicians to play. His face went terribly pale and he began to tremble as if from fever; his eyes gleamed with a strange fire; he smoothed back his black hair with one hand, wiped beads of sweat from his high forehead with a handkerchief, and suddenly strode forward, folding his arms across his chest. The music died away. The improvisation began.

> *The palace shines. Sweet melodies,*
> *Accompanied by flute and lyre,*
> *And her sweet voice, and her bright eyes,*
> *Make light of dark, make night expire.*
> *All hearts bow down towards her throne;*
> *She is the Queen whom all must court –*
> *But then her own fair head sinks down*
> *Towards her golden cup in thought.*

Flutes, lyres and voices – all goes dead.
A deepening silence fills the hall.
But when once more she lifts her head,
Her words both frighten and enthral:
'My love holds bliss, so I keep hearing.
If there is truth in what you claim,
Blessed is he his whose love has daring
Enough to pay the price I name.
My contract binds all equally:
He who would claim me as his wife,
He who desires one night with me,
Must for that night lay down his life.

'Once I lie on the bed of pleasure –
I swear by all the gods above –
I'll bring delight beyond all measure
Yet be the humblest slave of love.
Hear me, O splendid Aphrodite,
And you, dread God who reigns below,
And you above, great Zeus almighty –
I swear: until the dawn's first glow
Brightens the sky, I shall divine
Each hidden wish of my lord's heart;
I'll set on fire, then soothe with wine;
I'll bare the mysteries of love's art.
But when the Eastern sky turns red, .
When my lord feels the morning's breath,
Soldiers will lead him from my bed
To meet the lasting kiss of death.'

All hearts rebel, and yet they all
Remain enslaved by beauty's charm.
Uncertain murmurs fill the hall;
She listens with untroubled calm
And looks around with haughty pride,
Thinking her suitors spurn her offer.

Then one emerges from the crowd;
Two others follow quickly after.
Their steps are bold, their eyes are bright;
She rises to her feet to meet them.
The bargain's struck; each buys one night,
And when it's over, death will greet them.

The lovers' lots are blessed by priests
And dropped inside the fateful urn.
Then, watched in silence by the guests,
A lot is drawn. First comes the turn,
The gods decree, of gallant Flavius,
Flavius whose courage never wavers.
Such scorn in a mere woman's eyes
Is more than Flavius can endure;
Amazed by Cleopatra's gall,
This grey-haired veteran of war
Now leaps to answer pleasure's call
As once he answered battle cries.
Criton comes next, a youthful sage
Born in the groves of Epicure,
Whose graceful verses sing the rage
Induced by Venus and Amor.
The third is like a glowing rose
Whose petals dawn has coaxed apart,
A joy to both the eye and heart,
A youth whose name the centuries
Have lost. The softest shadow lies
Over his cheeks; love fills his eyes.
The passions raging in his breast
Are like a still-closed book to him
And Cleopatra looks at him
With eyes surprised by tenderness.

NOTES

1.'Who is that man?' 'Oh, he's someone very talented. He can make his voice do anything.'
'He'd do well, madam, to make himself a new pair of trousers with it.'

2. 'Signor… please excuse me if…'

3. 'I believed… I thought… Your Excellency will forgive me…'

4. No doubt because of the censorship, Pushkin deleted the original continuation of this
sentence: 'and all they ask from Maecenases (the devil take them) is that they should not
secretly denounce them (and not even this wish is granted)'. Gaius Maecenas (d.8 BC)
was a wealthy and prominent patron of the arts under the Emperor Augustus; he
commissioned patriotic and propagandistic works from the likes of Virgil and Horace.

5. By Jove!

6. The thought in this sentence is borrowed from a sonnet by Michelangelo.

7. An opera by Rossini (1792–1868), written in 1813.

8. The last day of Pompeii. Cleopatra and her lovers. Spring seen from a prison. The
triumph of Tasso.

9. Since the great queen had many of them.

Alexander Sergeevich Pushkin was born in Moscow in 1799 into an aristocratic but impoverished family. His mother was the grand-daughter of Peter the Great's Abyssinian Engineer-General. The young Pushkin was educated in French, but learnt his native Russian from household servants. He attended the Imperial Lyceum at Tsarskoye Selo, and, at the age of fifteen, published his first poem. By the time he had graduated from the Lyceum at the age of eighteen, Pushkin was already an acknowledged force in contemporary literature.

In 1817, Pushkin took up a post in the Ministry of Foreign Affairs at St Petersburg. Here he lived a riotous existence, and became involved with a group of young men who later formed part of the Decembrist uprising of 1825. His writing took on a more seditious flavour, and in 1820 his political poem 'On Liberty' drew the attention of the authorities and led to his banishment from St Petersburg. Pushkin was moved south to the Caucasus, where he was to remain for three years, and where he read the work of Byron for the first time. In 1823, Pushkin was moved to Odessa, a more pleasant place of exile, where to some extent he was able to resume his former life. It was here that he began his greatest work *Eugene Onegin* (1823–31). The following year, however, he was again moved – after the interception of some correspondence – this time to his mother's estate in Mikhailovskoye, where he was kept under guard.

Despite the unsettled nature of his life in the 1820s, Pushkin continued to write, and his reputation gradually grew. When Tsar Alexander I was assassinated in 1825, the new Tsar, Nicholas I, recognised Pushkin's great popularity and, in 1827, his exile was finally revoked. He settled in St Petersburg where he met and fell in love with Natalya Nikolayevna Goncharova, a beautiful young aristocrat, whom he married in 1831.

In the early 1830s, Pushkin wrote and published several poems, plays and short stories, including *Boris Godunov*, *Mozart and Salieri* and *The Queen of Spades*. He found, however, that the Tsar's sponsorship, rather than increasing his literary freedom, led to a more severe censorship. Added to this frustration was that of his marriage, which was becoming increasingly unhappy due to Natalya's extravagant tastes and open flirtations. In 1836 a public scandal was caused by her affair with Baron Georges d'Anthès. Pushkin challenged d'Anthès to a duel in defence of his wife's honour. The duel took place in January 1837, and Pushkin was severely wounded. He died two days later.

Robert Chandler's poems have appeared in the *Times Literary Supplement* and *Poetry Review*. His translations of Sappho and Apollinaire have been published in the *Everyman's Poetry* series, and he has been a regular contributor for many years to the journal *Modern Poetry in Translation*. He is the translator of Vasily Grossman's 'Life and Fate', and the co-translator of five volumes of the work of Andrey Platonov.

SELECTED TITLES FROM HESPERUS PRESS

Gustave Flaubert *Memoirs of a Madman*

Alexander Pope *Scriblerus*

Ugo Foscolo *Last Letters of Jacopo Ortis*

Anton Chekhov *The Story of a Nobody*

Joseph von Eichendorff *Life of a Good-for-nothing*

Mark Twain *The Diary of Adam and Eve*

Giovanni Boccaccio *Life of Dante*

Victor Hugo *The Last Day of a Condemned Man*

Joseph Conrad *Heart of Darkness*

Edgar Allan Poe *Eureka*

Emile Zola *For a Night of Love*

Daniel Defoe *The King of Pirates*

Giacomo Leopardi *Thoughts*

Nikolai Gogol *The Squabble*

Franz Kafka *Metamorphosis*

Herman Melville *The Enchanted Isles*

Leonardo da Vinci *Prophecies*

Charles Baudelaire *On Wine and Hashish*

William Makepeace Thackeray *Rebecca and Rowena*

Wilkie Collins *Who Killed Zebedee?*

Théophile Gautier *The Jinx*

Charles Dickens *The Haunted House*

Luigi Pirandello *Loveless Love*

Fyodor Dostoevsky *Poor People*

E.T.A. Hoffmann *Mademoiselle de Scudéri*

Henry James *In the Cage*

Francis Petrarch *My Secret Book*

André Gide *Theseus*

D.H. Lawrence *The Fox*

Percy Bysshe Shelley *Zastrozzi*

Marquis de Sade *Incest*

Oscar Wilde *The Portrait of Mr W.H.*

Giacomo Casanova *The Duel*

Leo Tolstoy *Hadji Murat*